Captain Nemo's Fantastic Voyage

20,000 Leagues Under the Sea

by JULES VERNE

Abridged and Edited by Vic Crume

SCHOLASTIC INC.
New York Toronto London Auckland Sydney Tokyo

ISBN 0-590-05811-8

16 15 14 13 12 11 10 9 8 7 6   4 5 6 7 8/8

Printed in the U.S.A.   01

CONTENTS

PART II

PART I

A SHIFTING REEF

THE YEAR 1866 was marked by a series of remarkable incidents, and a mysterious phenomenon that excited people everywhere. It affected seafaring men particularly — shiping merchants, common sailors, ships' captains, skippers and officers of the American as well as many European navies. Their governments were equally concerned.

For some time past, vessels on the high seas had reported sighting "an enormous thing," a long, spindle-shaped object, occasionally phosphorescent, and infinitely larger and more rapid in its movements than a whale.

The facts relating to this apparition (entered in various logbooks) agreed in most respects as to the shape of the object or creature, the untiring rapidity of its movements, its surprising power of locomotion, and the peculiar life with which it seemed endowed. If it was a species of whale, it surpassed in size all those classified by scientists. Some reported it as 200 feet long. Others claimed it was a mile in width by three in length. Taking all their various estimates into consideration, one might fairly conclude that this mysterious being must be much larger than any living creature known to science.

On the 20th of July 1866, the steamer *Governor Higginson,* of the Calcutta and Burnach Steam Navigation Company, had met this moving mass five miles off the east coast of Australia. Captain Baker prepared to determine its exact position, when two columns of water shot up with a hissing noise 150 feet into the air.

Similar facts were observed on the 23rd of July in the Pacific Ocean, by the *Columbus,* of the West India and Pacific Steam Navigation Company.

This extraordinary cetaceous creature could transport itself from one place to another with surprising velocity — as, in an interval of three days, the *Governor Higginson* and the *Columbus* had observed it at two different points of the chart, separated by a distance of more than 700 nautical leagues.

Fifteen days later and 2000 miles farther off, the *Helvetia*, of the Compagnie-Nationale, and the *Shannon*, of the Royal Mail Steamship Company, were in the North Atlantic when they signaled the monster to each other in 42° 15′ N. lat. and 60° 35′ W. long. They estimated the minimum length of the mammal as more than 350 feet.

Now even the largest whales — those which frequent those parts of the sea around the Aleutian, Kulammak, and Umgullich islands — have never exceeded the length of 180 feet, if they attain that.

These reports, arriving one after the other with fresh observations made on board transatlantic ships, greatly influenced public opinion. Light-thinking people jested about the phenomenon, but governments of countries, such as England, America, and Germany, treated the matter more seriously.

Everywhere, people sang of the monster in the cafés, ridiculed it in the newspapers, and represented it on the stage. All kinds of stories were circulated regarding it. There appeared in the papers caricatures of every gigantic and imaginary creature, from the white whale, the terrible "Moby Dick," to the immense kraken, whose tentacles could entangle a ship of 500 tons and hurry it into the abyss of the ocean.

Soon, "the question of the monster" inflamed all minds, and editors of scientific journals, quarreled with believers in the supernatural.

For six months war was waged in leading science journals. Then, during the first months of the year 1867, when the matter seemed buried, never to revive, new facts were brought before the public. It was now no longer a scientific problem to be solved, but a real danger seriously to be avoided. The question took quite another shape. The monster became a small island, a rock, a reef, but a reef of indefinite and shifting proportions.

On the 5th of March 1867, the *Moravian*, of the Montreal Ocean Company, in 27° 30' lat. and 72° 15' long., struck on her starboard quarter a rock, marked on no chart for that part of the sea. Had it not been for the hull's superior strength, the *Moravian* would have been broken by the shock and gone down with the 237 passengers she was bringing home from Canada.

On the 13th of April 1867, in a calm sea, the *Scotia*, of the Cunard Company's line, was in 15° 12' long. and 45° 37' lat., moving at the speed of thirteen and a half knots.

At seventeen minutes past four in the afternoon, while the passengers were assembled at tea, a slight shock was felt on the hull of the *Scotia*.

The *Scotia* had not struck, but she had *been* struck, and seemingly by something sharp and penetrating. The shock had been so slight that no one would have been alarmed, had it not been for the carpenter, who rushed onto the bridge, exclaiming, "We are sinking! We are sinking!"

At first the passengers were much frightened, but Captain Anderson hastened to reassure them. The *Scotia* was divided into seven compartments by strong partitions.

Captain Anderson went down immediately into the hold. He found that the sea was pouring into the fifth compartment. Fortunately, this compartment did not hold the boilers, or the fires would have been immediately extinguished. He ordered the engines to be stopped at once. Some minutes afterward they discovered a large hole in the ship's side. Such a leak could not be repaired at sea. The *Scotia* continued her course and after three days' delay entered Liverpool harbor.

The *Scotia* was put in dry dock and engineers found that the hole, $2\frac{1}{2}$ yards below water mark, was in the shape of an isosceles triangle. It was clear that the instrument producing the perforation had been driven with prodigious strength to pierce the iron plate 1⅜ inches thick!

From this moment on, all unlucky casualties which could not be otherwise accounted for were put down to the monster. It was held responsible for all these shipwrecks, and thanks to the fears it aroused, communication between continents became more and more difficult. The public demanded that the seas should at any price be rid of this formidable creature.

PRO AND CON

At the period when these events took place, I had just returned from a scientific research in the territory of Nebraska, in the United States. As an assistant professor in the Museum of Natural History in Paris, I had been sent on that expedition by the French government.

I arrived in New York toward the end of March, laden with a precious collection. My departure for France was fixed for the first days in May. I was occupying myself in classifying my mineralogical, botanical, and zoological riches, when the accident to the *Scotia* occurred.

Of course I was interested. The subject of

the monster was the issue of the day. I had read and reread all the American and European papers without being any nearer to a conclusion about it. The mystery intrigued me, and I jumped from one opinion to the other. For there were only two possibilities: either it was a monster of colossal strength, or a submarine vessel of enormous motive power.

That a private gentleman should have such a machine at his command was not likely. Where, when, and how was it built? How could its construction have been kept secret? Certainly a government might possess such a destructive machine. But after inquiries made in government circles in England, France, Russia, Germany, Spain, Italy, America, and even in Turkey, the idea of an underwater vessel — a submarine — was definitely rejected.

Upon my arrival in New York several persons did me the honor of consulting me on the phenomenon in question. I had published two volumes, entitled, *Mysteries of the Great Submarine Grounds*. This book had gained for me a special reputation in this branch of natural history. My advice was asked, and as "the Honorable Pierre Aronnax, Professor in the Museum of Paris," I was called upon by the *New York Herald* to express a definite opinion of some sort. I give here an extract from the article which I published the 30th of April. It ran as follows:

"After rejecting all other suggestions, it becomes necessary to admit the existence of a marine animal of enormous power.

"The great depths of the ocean are entirely unknown to us. Soundings cannot reach them. What beings live, or can live, twelve or fifteen miles beneath the surface of the waters we can scarcely guess. If Nature still has ocean secrets for us, nothing is more reasonable than to admit the existence of unknown fishes, or whales — even of new species.

"We must necessarily seek for the animal in question among those marine beings already classed. And in that case, I should be disposed to admit the existence of a gigantic narwhal.

"A species of whale, the common narwhal, or unicorn of the sea, often attains a length of 60 feet. Increase its size tenfold, give it strength proportionate to its size, lengthen its destructive weapons, and you obtain the animal with power necessary to pierce the hull of the steamer.

"Indeed, the narwhal is armed with a sort of ivory sword. The principal tusk has the hardness of steel. Some of these tusks have been found buried in the bodies of whales, which the 'unicorn' always attacks with success. Others have been drawn out from the bottoms of ships, which they have pierced through and through, as a gimlet pierces a barrel. The Museum of the Faculty of Medicine of Paris possesses one of these defensive weapons, 2¼ yards in length, and 15 inches in diameter at the base.

"Now suppose this weapon to be six times stronger, and the animal ten times more powerful. Launch it at the rate of 20 miles an hour and you obtain a shock capable of producing the damage to the *Scotia*. Until further information, therefore, I shall maintain it to be a 'sea-unicorn' of colossal dimensions, armed with a real spur, like the armored frigates or 'rams' of war, whose massiveness and motive power it would possess at the same time. Thus may this phenomenon be explained, unless there is something beyond what anyone has ever imagined, seen, perceived or experienced."

My article was warmly discussed. The solution it proposed gave, at least, full liberty to the imagination. The human mind delights in grand conceptions of supernatural beings.

The United States was the first to outfit an expedition destined to pursue this narwhal.

A frigate of great speed, the *Abraham Lincoln*, was quickly put into commission in New York harbor, and Commander Farragut hastened the arming of his frigate.

But as soon as it was decided to pursue the

monster, the monster seemed to disappear. For two months no one heard about it. No ship met with it — almost as if this "unicorn" knew of the plot against it.

Then on the 2nd of July, it was learned that a steamer bound from San Francisco to Shanghai had sighted the animal three weeks before in the North Pacific Ocean!

Three hours before the *Abraham Lincoln* left the pier, I received a letter worded as follows:

To M. ARONNAX,
 Professor in the Museum of Paris,
Fifth Avenue Hotel, New York.
      Sir: If you will consent to join the *Abraham Lincoln* in this expedition, the Government of the United States will with pleasure see France represented in the enterprise. Commander Farragut has a cabin at your disposal.
                              Very cordially yours,
                                  J. B. HOBSON,
                              Secretary of Marine.

Three seconds before the arrival of J. B. Hobson's letter, I had no more thought of pursuing the "unicorn" than of attempting the passage of the North Sea. Three seconds after reading the letter of the Honorable Secretary of Marine, I felt that the sole end of my life was to chase this disturbing monster and purge it from the world.

"Conseil," I called, in an impatient voice.

Conseil, my Flemish servant, accompanied me in all my travels. I liked him, and he liked me. He was very quick, apt at any service required of him, and, despite his name, never giving advice — even when asked for it.

Conseil had followed me for the last ten years wherever science led. Never once did he complain of the length or fatigue of a journey, never made an objection to pack up for whatever country it might be, or however far away, whether China or the Congo. Besides all this he had good health, which defied all sickness, solid muscles, and no nerves.

"Conseil," said I again, beginning with feverish hands to make preparations for my departure.

Conseil appeared.

"Did you call, sir?" said he, entering.

"Yes. Make preparations for me and yourself too. We leave in two hours."

"As you please, sir," replied Conseil, quietly.

"Not an instant to lose! Pack all traveling needs — coats, shirts and socks — as many as you can, and make haste."

"And your Nebraska collections, sir?"

"We will think of them by and by, and I will

give orders to forward our collection to France."

"We are not returning to Paris, then," said Conseil.

"Oh! certainly," I answered, evasively, "by making a curve."

"Will the curve please you, sir."

"Oh! it will be nothing — not quite so direct a way, that is all. We will take passage on the *Abraham Lincoln*."

"As you think proper, sir," coolly replied Conseil.

"You see, my friend, it has to do with the monster — the famous narwhal. We are going to purge it from the seas. The author of the *Mysteries of the Great Submarine Grounds* cannot forbear embarking with Commander Farragut. A glorious mission, but a dangerous one! We cannot tell where we may go. But we have a good captain."

Once aboard the frigate, I asked for Commander Farragut. One of the sailors conducted me to the poop, where a fine-looking officer held out his hand to me.

"Professor Pierre Aronnax?" said he.

"Himself," I replied. "Commander Farragut?"

"You are welcome, Professor. Your cabin is ready for you."

The *Abraham Lincoln* had been well chosen and equipped for her new destination. She was a frigate of great speed, fitted with high-pressure engines.

The interior arrangement of the frigate corresponded to its nautical qualities. I was well satisfied with my cabin.

"We shall be well off here," said I to Conseil. Then I left him to stow our trunks conveniently away, and remounted the deck to watch the preparations for departure.

At that moment Commander Farragut was ordering the last moorings to be cast loose which held the *Abraham Lincoln* to the pier of Brooklyn. So in a quarter of an hour, perhaps less, the frigate would have sailed without me. I should have missed this extraordinary, supernatural, and incredible expedition!

Six bells struck, the pilot got into his boat and rejoined the little schooner which was waiting under our lee. The fires were stoked, the screw propellers churned the waves, and soon the frigate was skirting the low coast of Long Island. At eight bells, having lost sight of the lights of Fire Island, we steamed into the dark waters of the Atlantic.

THE VOYAGE OF THE ABRAHAM LINCOLN

CAPTAIN FARRAGUT was a good seaman, worthy of the frigate he commanded. His vessel and he were one, and he was the soul of it. On the question of the cetacean there was no doubt in his mind, and he would not allow the existence of the animal to be disputed on board. Either Captain Farragut would kill the narwhal, or the narwhal would kill the captain. There was no third course.

The officers on board shared the opinion of their chief. They were ever chatting, discussing and calculating the various chances of a meeting, watching narrowly the vast surface of the ocean. More than one took up his quarters voluntarily in the cross-trees, and the rigging was crowded with sailors. They watched the sea eagerly, as Captain Farragut had spoken of a certain sum of 2000 dollars, set apart for whoever should first sight the monster, were he cabin boy, common seaman, or officer.

The *Abraham Lincoln* was equipped with every means of destruction. And, what was better still, we had on board Ned Land, the prince of harpooners.

Ned Land, a Canadian with an uncommon quickness of hand, knew no equal in his dangerous occupation. Skill, coolness, audacity and cunning he possessed in a superior degree, and it must be a cunning whale to escape the stroke of his harpoon.

Ned Land was more than 6 feet tall, strongly built, grave and silent, and occasionally violent when contradicted. The harpooner's family was originally from Quebec — a tribe of hardy fishermen when that town belonged to France.

I am portraying my companion as I really knew him. (We are old friends now, united in that unchangeable friendship which is born and cemented amidst extreme dangers.)

Now, what was Ned Land's opinion upon the question of the marine monster? I must admit that he did not believe in the unicorn, and was the only one on board who did not share that universal conviction. He avoided the subject.

One magnificent evening about three weeks after our departure, the frigate was abreast of Cape Blanc, 30 miles to leeward of the coast of Patagonia. We had crossed the Tropic of Capricorn, and the Straits of Magellan opened less than 700 miles to the south. In eight days the *Abraham Lincoln* would be ploughing the waters of the Pacific.

Seated on the poop, Ned Land and I were chatting of one thing and another as we looked at this mysterious sea, whose great depths had always been inaccessible to the eye of man. I naturally led up the conversation to the giant unicorn.

"Well, Ned," said I, "is it possible that you are not convinced of the existence of the cetacean that we are following? Have you any particular reason for being so incredulous?"

The harpooner looked at me fixedly for some moments before answering. "Perhaps I have, Professor. As a whaler I have followed many a cetacean, harpooned a great number and killed several. But however strong or well-armed they have been, neither their tails nor their weapons would have been able even to scratch the iron plates of a steamer."

"But, Ned, they tell of ships which the tusk of the narwhal has pierced through and through."

23

"Wooden ships — that is possible," replied the Canadian; "but until further proof, I deny that whales, other cetaceans, or sea-unicorns could ever produce the effect you describe."

"Well, Ned, I do believe in the existence of a mammal powerfully organized, belonging to the branch of vertebrata like the whales, and with a horn of defense of great penetrating power."

"Hum!" said the harpooner, shaking his head with the air of a man who would not be convinced.

"Consider one thing, my worthy Canadian," I resumed. "If such an animal is in existence, if it inhabits the depths of the ocean, if it frequents the strata lying miles below the surface of the water where the pressure is so very great, then it must necessarily possess great strength."

"Why!" exclaimed Ned Land, "they must have iron plates 8 inches thick!"

"As you say, Ned. And think what destruction such a mass would cause, if hurled with the speed of an express train against the hull of a vessel."

"Yes — certainly — perhaps," replied the Canadian, shaken by these figures, but not yet willing to give in.

"Well, have I convinced you?"

"You have convinced me of one thing, sir, which is that, if such animals do exist at the bottom of the seas, they must necessarily be as strong as you say."

"But if they do *not* exist, how explain the accident to the *Scotia*?" I asked.

The voyage of the *Abraham Lincoln* was for a long time marked by no special incident.

The 6th of July, about three o'clock in the afternoon, the *Abraham Lincoln* rounded Cape Horn. The course was toward the northwest, and the next day the screw of the frigate was churning the waters of the Pacific.

On the 20th of July, we cut the Tropic of Capricorn at 105° long., and on the 27th of the same month we crossed the equator on the 100th meridian. After that, the frigate steered a decidedly more westerly course, through the central waters of the Pacific. Commander Farragut thought it better for our search to remain in deep water and stay clear of continents or islands. The frigate crossed the Tropic of Cancer and made for the China Seas.

We were now in the area where the monster had last been seen, and the crew was in a state of nervous excitement. Twenty times a day a sailor would imagine he saw the monster. The excitement mounted to fever pitch.

But then for several weeks, during which every day seemed an age, the *Abraham Lincoln* furrowed the waters of the Northern Pacific — all in vain. We saw no monster, only harmless whales. There was bound to be a reaction among the crew to what now seemed a useless search.

I will not say there was a mutiny on board, but after a reasonable period of obstinacy, Captain Farragut — as Columbus did — asked for three days' patience. If in three days the monster did not appear, the man at the helm should give three turns of the wheel, and the *Abraham Lincoln* would make for European seas.

This promise was made on the 2nd of November. It had the effect of rallying the crew, and they watched the ocean with renewed attention.

Two days passed; the steam was at half pressure. A thousand schemes were tried to attract the attention and stimulate the apathy of the animal in case it should still be in those parts. Large quantities of bacon were trailed in the wake of the ship — to the great satisfaction of the sharks.

The next day, the 5th of November, at twelve, Commander Farragut was to turn the course to the southeast and abandon forever the regions of the Pacific.

The frigate was then in 31° 15′ N. lat. and 136° 42′ E. long. The coast of Japan was less than 200 miles to leeward. Night was approaching; the ship had just struck eight bells. Clouds veiled the moon, and the sea rolled peacefully under the vessel.

At that moment I was leaning forward on the starboard netting. Conseil was standing near me, looking straight ahead. Members of the crew, perched in the ratlines, scoured the darkening horizon, while officers with their night glasses searched the growing darkness. Suddenly, in the midst of general silence, a voice was heard. It was Ned Land shouting:

"Look out there! The very thing we are looking for — on our weather beam!"

AT FULL STEAM

At THIS CRY the whole ship's crew hurried
toward the harpooner — commander, officers,
sailors, cabin boy, and even the engineer and
stokers.

Ned Land was not mistaken. At two cables'
length from the *Abraham Lincoln,* on the starboard quarter, the sea itself seemed to be alight.
The monster was evidently submerged some
fathoms below the surface, but threw out that
very intense light mentioned in the reports of
several captains. It must have been produced
by an agent of great *shining* power. The luminous part traced on the sea an immense oval,
whose center burned with a white-hot intensity
that faded outward into the darkness.

28

"It is nothing more than a mass of phosphorescent particles," said one of the officers.

"No!" I cried. "That brightness comes from some electrical source. Now it is moving forward . . . backward . . . it is darting toward us!"

"Up helm; reverse the engines!" cried the captain.

The frigate moved rapidly away from the burning light, but the thing came after us at double our velocity. We gasped for breath as the animal gained rapidly on us, cresting the waves. The monster circled the frigate, which was then making 14 knots, and enveloped us with its electric rays.

It moved off two or three miles, then all at once, from the dark line of the horizon, the monster rushed suddenly toward the *Abraham Lincoln*. It stopped about 20 feet from our hull. The light died out and it disappeared. Then it suddenly reappeared on the other side of the vessel, as if it had turned and slid under the hull. The frigate fled rather than attack.

On the captain's face, generally so impassive, was an expression of astonishment.

"Professor Aronnax," he said, "I do not know with what formidable being I have to deal, and I will not risk my frigate in the darkness. How we can attack this unknown thing, how defend ourselves, will be clearer in day-light."

"You have no further doubt, Captain, of the nature of the animal?"

"No, sir. It is evidently a gigantic narwhal, and an electric one. And if it possesses such dreadful power, it is the most terrible animal that ever was created."

No one thought of sleep that night. The *Abraham Lincoln* cruised at half speed. The monster, imitating the frigate, moved lazily at our speed, but it seemed determined not to leave the scene. Toward midnight, however, it disappeared, or "died out" like a large glow-worm. Had it fled? One could only fear, not hope. But at seven minutes to one o'clock in the morning a deafening whistling was heard, like that produced by a body of water rushing with great violence.

The captain, Ned Land and I were then on deck, striving to pierce the profound darkness.

"Ned Land," asked the commander, "you have often heard the roaring of whales?"

"Often, sir. But never such whales as this one, the sight of which brought me in 2000 dollars. If I can only get within four harpoon lengths of it!"

"But to approach it," said the commander, "I ought to put a whaler at your disposal?"

"Certainly, sir."

"That will be trifling with the lives of my men."

"And mine too," said the harpooner simply.

Toward two o'clock in the morning, the burning light reappeared, not less intense, about 5 miles to windward of the *Abraham Lincoln*. Notwithstanding the distance, and the noise of the wind and sea, one heard distinctly the loud strokes of the animal's tail, and even its panting breath. It seemed at that moment that the monster narwhal had come to breathe at the surface of the water. The air was engulfed in its lungs, like the steam in the vast cylinders of a machine of 2000 horse-power.

At six o'clock, day began to break, and the electric light of the narwhal disappeared. At seven o'clock a thick sea fog obscured our view and the best spyglasses could not pierce it. That caused disappointment and anger.

I climbed the mizzen mast. Some officers were already perched on the mast heads. At eight o'clock the fog lay heavily on the waves, its thick scrolls rising little by little. The horizon widened as the fog cleared. Suddenly, just as on the day before, Ned Land's voice was heard:

"The thing is on the port quarter!"

31

Every eye was turned toward that point. There, a mile and a half from the frigate, a long blackish body was emerging from the waves.

The frigate approached the cetacean, and I examined the creature thoroughly, estimating its length at 250 feet. As I watched, it ejected two jets of steam and water from its vents, and its body rose to the height of 120 feet.

The crew waited impatiently for orders. The captain, after having observed the animal attentively, called to the engineer.

"Sir," said the commander, "is the pressure up?"

"Yes, sir," answered the engineer.

"Well, stoke your fires and then full steam ahead."

The time had now come for the fateful battle with the monster! A few minutes later, the funnels of the frigate vomited clouds of black smoke, and the bridge trembled with the power of the boilers.

The *Abraham Lincoln* headed straight toward the creature, which allowed the frigate to come within half a cable's length. Then it turned and stopped a short distance off.

This pursuit lasted nearly three-quarters of an hour, without the frigate gaining a yard on the cetacean. It was quite evident that at that rate we should never catch up with it.

"Well, Mr. Land," asked the captain, "do you advise me to put the boats out to sea?"

"No, sir," replied Ned Land, "because we shall not take that beast easily."

"What shall we do then?"

"Put on more steam if you can, sir. With your leave, I mean to post myself under the bowsprit, and if we get within harpooning distance I shall throw my harpoon."

"Good," said the captain. "Engineer, more pressure."

The fires were stoked to capacity, and Ned Land went to his post.

We calculated that the frigate was moving at the rate of 18.5 knots. But the accursed animal swam at the same speed. For an hour we kept up the pace without gaining on the monster. It was humiliating for one of the swiftest ships in the American navy. A stubborn anger seized the crew. They shouted curses at the elusive creature, and the captain gnawed his moustache in frustration.

The engineer was again summoned.

"You have a full head of steam up?"

"Yes, sir," replied the engineer.

"Well, increase the pressure."

With that the *Abraham Lincoln*'s speed increased to 19.5 knots. The masts trembled, and clouds of smoke poured out of the narrow funnels.

What a pursuit! We were beside ourselves with excitement. Ned Land kept his post, harpoon in hand. "We're gaining! We shall capture it!" cried the brave Canadian.

But just as he was about to strike, the cetacean moved rapidly away. Even with our maximum speed, the thing outmaneuvered our ship, circling around and around us. At that, a cry of fury rose from us all!

At noon we had made no further advance on the thing than we'd had at eight o'clock that morning.

The captain then decided to take more direct action.

"So!" said he, "the animal is faster than the *Abraham Lincoln*. Very well! We will see whether it will escape these conical bullets. Send your men to the forecastle, sir."

The forecastle gun was immediately loaded and slewed around. But the shot passed some feet above the cetacean, which was half a mile off.

"Another volley, more to the right," cried the commander, "and five dollars to whoever hits that infernal beast."

An old gunner with a gray beard, a steady eye and a grave face, went up to the gun and took a long aim. A loud report was heard, mingled with the cheers of the crew.

The bullet did its work; it hit the animal, but not fatally, and sliding off its rounded surface, was lost in the two-mile depth of sea.

The chase began again, and the captain leaning toward me, said:

"I will pursue that beast till my frigate blows up."

"Yes," answered I, "and you will be quite right to do it."

I wished the beast would tire itself out, but hours passed without its showing any signs of exhaustion. Then night came on, and we saw no sign of the monster's mysterious light.

Now, I thought, our expedition is at an end. We will never again see the extraordinary animal.

I was mistaken. At ten minutes to eleven in the evening the strange light reappeared 3 miles to windward of the frigate, as pure, as intense as during the preceding night.

The narwhal seemed motionless — tired perhaps, with its day's work — and floated with the waves. Now was our chance to take advantage!

The captain gave his orders. The *Abraham*

Lincoln kept up half steam. It is not rare to meet in the middle of the ocean whales so sound asleep that they can be successfully attacked, and Ned Land had harpooned more than one during its sleep. The Canadian went to take his place under the bowsprit.

The frigate approached noiselessly and stopped at two cables' length from the animal. No one breathed. A deep silence reigned on the bridge. We were not a hundred feet from the burning focus, whose light increased and dazzled our eyes.

At this moment, leaning on the forecastle bulwark, I saw below me Ned Land brandishing his terrible harpoon scarcely 20 feet from the motionless animal. Suddenly his arm straightened, and the harpoon was thrown. I heard the stroke of the weapon, which seemed to have struck a hard body. The electric light went out suddenly, and two enormous waterspouts broke over the bridge of the frigate, rushing like a torrent from stem to stern, overthrowing men and breaking the lashing of the spars. A fearful shock followed, and, thrown over the rail without having time to stop myself, I fell into the sea!

AN UNKNOWN SPECIES OF WHALE

THIS FALL so stunned me that I have no
clear recollection of my sensations. I was at
first drawn down to a depth of about 20 feet.
I am a good swimmer and so I did not panic.
Two vigorous strokes brought me to the surface of the water, and my first care was to
look for the frigate. Had the crew seen me disappear? Had the *Abraham Lincoln* veered
round? Would the captain put out a boat?
Might I hope to be saved?

The darkness was intense, but I caught a
glimpse of a black mass disappearing in the
east, its beacon lights dying out in the distance. It was the frigate! I was lost.

"Help! help!" I shouted, swimming toward
the *Abraham Lincoln* in desperation.

My clothes seemed glued to my body, and they paralyzed my movements.

I was sinking! I was suffocating!

"Help!"

This was my last cry. My mouth filled with water. I struggled against being drawn down into the abyss. Suddenly my clothes were seized by a strong hand, and I felt myself drawn up to the surface of the sea. And I heard, yes, I heard these words: "If master would be so good as to lean on my shoulder, master would swim with much greater ease."

I seized with one hand my faithful Conseil's arm.

"Is it you?" said I, "you?"

"Myself," answered Conseil; "and waiting master's orders."

"That shock threw you as well as me into the sea?"

"No. But being in my master's service, I followed him."

The worthy fellow thought that was but natural.

"And the frigate?" I asked.

"The frigate?" replied Conseil, turning on his back. "I think that master had better not count too much on her."

"You think so?"

"I say that because at the time I threw myself into the sea, I heard the men at the wheel say, 'The screw and the rudder are broken.'"

"Broken?"

"Yes, broken by the monster's teeth. The ship no longer answers her helm. She cannot turn back."

"Then we are lost!"

"Perhaps so," calmly answered Conseil. "However, we have still several hours before us, and one can do a good deal in some hours."

Conseil's coolness set me up again. I swam more vigorously. But, cramped by my clothes, which stuck to me like a leaden weight, I felt great difficulty in bearing up. Conseil saw this.

"Will master let me make a slit?" said he. And slipping an open knife under my outer clothes, he ripped them and slipped them off me.

Then I did the same for Conseil, and we continued to swim. We decided that our only chance of safety was being picked up by the *Abraham Lincoln's* boats. We ought to manage to wait for them as long as possible. While one of us lay on our back, quite still, with arms crossed and legs stretched out, the other would swim and push the other on in front. This towing business did not last more than ten minutes for each, and relieving each other thus, we could swim on for some hours, perhaps till daybreak.

The collision of the frigate with the cetacean had occurred about eleven o'clock the evening before. I reckoned then we should have eight hours to swim before sunrise, an operation quite practicable if we relieved each other. The sea, very calm, was in our favor. Sometimes I tried to pierce the intense darkness that was only slightly lessened by the phosphorescence in the water. I watched the luminous waves that broke over my hand. Their mirror-like surface was spotted with silvery rings. One might have said that we were in a bath of quicksilver.

Near one o'clock in the morning, I was seized with dreadful cramps. "Leave me! Leave me!" I said to Conseil.

"Leave my master? Never!" replied he. "I would drown first."

Just then the moon appeared through the clouds. The surface of the sea glittered with its rays, and I looked around at all the points of the horizon. I saw the frigate! She was five miles from us — and no boats!

I would have cried out. But what good would it have been at such a distance! Anyway, my swollen lips could utter no sounds.

I heard Conseil repeat at intervals — "Help!
Help!"

At one point we suspended our movements
for an instant and listened. It might have been
only a singing in the ear, but it seemed to me
as if a cry had answered the cry from Conseil.

"Did you hear?" I murmured.

"Yes! yes!"

And Conseil gave one more despairing call.

This time there was no mistake! A human
voice responded to ours! Was it the voice of
another unfortunate creature, abandoned in
the middle of the ocean, some other victim of
the shock sustained by the vessel? Or was it
a boat from the frigate, hailing us in the darkness?

Conseil made a last effort, and leaning on
my shoulder while I struck out in a despairing
effort, he raised himself half out of the water,
then fell backward exhausted.

"What did you see?"

"I saw — " he murmured. "I saw — "

What had he seen?

My strength was exhausted. My fingers
stiffened. My mouth filled with saltwater.
Cold crept over me. I raised my head for the
last time, then I sank.

At this moment a hard body struck me. I

clung to it. I felt that I was being drawn up, brought to the surface of the water. Then I fainted.

I soon came to, thanks to the vigorous rubbings that I received. I half opened my eyes.

"Conseil!" I murmured.

"Does master call me?" asked Conseil.

Just then, by the waning light of the moon, which was sinking down to the horizon, I saw a face which was not Conseil's and which I immediately recognized.

"Ned!" I cried. "Were you thrown into the sea by the shock of the frigate?"

"Yes, Professor; but more fortunate than you, I was able to find a footing almost directly upon a floating island."

"An island?"

"Or, more correctly speaking, on our gigantic narwhal."

"Explain, Ned!"

"And I soon found out why my harpoon was only blunted," he answered.

"Why, Ned, why?"

"Because, Professor, that beast is made of sheet iron."

The Canadian's last words produced a sudden revolution in my brain. Could Ned be right? I wiggled to the top of the object, half out of the water, which served us for a refuge.

I kicked it. The blow produced a metallic sound. Incredible though it might be, it seemed as if it *was* made of riveted plates.

There was no doubt about it! This monster, this natural phenomenon that had puzzled the learned world, and overthrown and misled the imagination of seamen of both hemispheres, was an even more astonishing phenomenon than they had dreamed, inasmuch as it was actually a human construction.

We were lying upon the back of a sort of submarine boat which looked like a huge fish of steel.

Just then a bubbling began at the back of this strange thing and it began to move. We had only just time to seize hold of the upper part, which rose about 7 feet out of the water, and happily its speed was not great.

"As long as it sails horizontally," muttered Ned Land, "I do not mind. But if it takes a fancy to dive, I would not give two straws for my life."

The Canadian was right, and it was necessary that we communicate as soon as possible with the beings, whatever they were, shut up inside the machine. I searched all over the outside for an entrance, but the lines of the iron rivets, solidly driven into the joints of the iron plates, were clear and uniform. Besides, the moon disappeared then, and left us in total darkness.

I can only recall one circumstance. During some lulls of the wind and sea, I fancied I heard several times vague sounds, a sort of fugitive harmony produced by distant words of command. What was then the mystery of this submarine craft, of which the whole world vainly sought an explanation? What kind of beings existed in this strange boat? What mechanical agent caused its prodigious speed?

Daybreak appeared. The morning mists surrounded us, but they soon cleared off. I was about to examine the hull, which formed on deck a kind of horizontal platform, when I felt it gradually sinking.

"Open!" cried Ned Land, kicking the resounding iron. "Open, you rascals!"

Happily the sinking movement ceased. Suddenly a noise, like iron works violently pushed aside, came from the interior of the boat. One iron plate was moved, a man appeared, uttered an odd cry, and disappeared immediately.

Some moments after, eight strong men, with masked faces, appeared noiselessly and drew us down into their formidable machine.

MOBILIS IN MOBILE — N.

THE NARROW PANEL closed upon us and we were again in darkness. My eyes, still dazzled by the outer light, could distinguish nothing. My naked feet clung to the rungs of an iron ladder. Ned Land and Conseil followed me down. When we reached the bottom of the ladder, a door opened into a room which we entered. Then the door shut after us with a bang.

We were alone. Where, I could not imagine. All was black, and so dense that even after some minutes, I could see nothing. But at least it was warm and dry.

Ned Land was furious at our imprisonment, calling our captors "north islanders for hospitality" and "maybe even cannibals."

"Calm yourself, friend Ned," I said to him. "Who can say for sure that they will not listen to us? Meanwhile let us try to find out where we are."

I groped about. In five steps I came to an iron wall, made of plates bolted together. Then, turning back, I struck against a wooden table, near which were ranged several stools. A thick carpet deadened the noise of our feet. Conseil, going round the reverse way, met me. The walls had revealed no trace of window or door, but we now knew that the room measured about 20 feet by 10. As to its height, even tall Ned Land could not touch the ceiling.

Half an hour passed without a change in our situation, when the dense darkness was suddenly dispelled by brilliant light. In its whiteness and intensity I recognized that same electric light which had played around the submarine boat. After shutting my eyes involuntarily, I opened them and saw that this light flooded down from the roof of the cabin.

"At last one can see," cried Ned Land. Knife in hand, he stood on the defensive.

"Yes," said I. "But we are still in the dark about ourselves."

"Let master have patience," said the imperturbable Conseil.

With the sudden lighting of the cabin, I saw

that it contained only the table and stools we had discovered earlier. We could hear no sound. All seemed dead in the interior of this boat. Did it move, did it still float on the surface of the ocean, or had it dived into the depths? I could not guess.

A noise of bolts was now heard. The door opened and two men appeared. One was short, muscular and broad-shouldered. He had an abundance of black hair, a thick moustache, and a quick penetrating look.

As to the second stranger, his head was well set on his shoulders and his black eyes looked around with calm, cold assurance. Whether this person was thirty-five or fifty years of age I could not say. He was tall, had a large forehead, a straight nose and a firm mouth. His eyes, set rather far apart, seemed to take in the whole scene at once.

The two strangers wore caps made from the fur of sea otters. They were shod with sea boots of seal's skin, and their fitted clothes were of a texture that allowed free movement of the limbs. The taller of the two, evidently the chief, examined us without saying a word. Then turning to his companion, he talked with him in a tongue unknown to us.

The other replied by a shake of the head. Then he seemed to question me by a look.

I replied in good French that I did not know his language. He seemed not to understand me.

"If master were to tell our story," said Conseil, "perhaps these gentlemen may understand *some* words."

I began to relate our adventures. I announced our names and rank, introducing myself, Conseil and Master Ned Land, the harpooner.

The man with the calm eyes listened to me with extreme attention. But nothing in his face indicated that he had understood my story. When I finished, he said not a word. There remained one resource, to speak English. Perhaps they would know this almost universal language.

"Go on in your turn," I said to the harpooner. "Speak your best English and try to do better than I."

To his great disgust, the harpooner could not make himself understood either. Our visitors spoke some words in their unknown language and left.

The door shut.

"My friends," I said, "we must not despair. We have been worse off than this. Do me the favor to wait a little before forming an opinion upon the commander and crew of this boat."

"My opinion is formed," replied Ned Land, sharply. "They are rascals."

As he said these words, the door opened. A steward entered. He brought us clothes — coats and trousers — made of a stuff I did not know. I hastened to dress myself, **an**d my companions followed my example. During that time, the steward — dumb, perhaps deaf — had arranged the table and laid three plates.

"This is something," said Conseil.

"Bah," said the harpooner, "what do you suppose they eat here? Tortoise liver, filet of shark, and beefsteaks from sea dogs?"

"We shall see," said Conseil.

The serving dishes, of bell metal, were placed on the table, and we took our places. Undoubtedly, I thought, we are dealing with civilized people. Had it not been for the electric light which flooded the room, I could have fancied I was in the dining room of the Grand Hotel in Paris. Among the dishes which were brought to us, I recognized several fish, and well prepared they were. But of some, although the flavor was excellent, I could give no opinion. Neither could I tell to what kingdom they belonged, whether animal or vegetable. As to the metal dinner service, it was elegant and in perfect taste. Each utensil, spoon, fork, knife, and plate had a letter engraved on it, with a motto above it, of which this is an exact facsimile:

MOBILIS IN MOBILI.

N.

The letter N was no doubt the last initial of the enigmatical person, who commanded at the bottom of the sea.

Ned and Conseil did not pause to reflect much. They devoured the food, and I did likewise. I was, besides, reassured as to our fate. And it seemed evident that our hosts would not let us die of want, at least.

However, everything has an end, even the hunger of people who have not eaten for fifteen hours. Our appetites satisfied, we felt overcome with sleep.

"Faith! I shall sleep well," said Conseil.

"So shall I," replied Ned Land.

My two companions stretched themselves on the cabin carpet, and were soon sound asleep. For my own part, too many thoughts crowded my brain. Too many questions pressed upon me, and too many fancies kept me awake. Where were we? What strange power carried us on? I felt — or rather fancied I felt — the machine sinking down to the lowest beds of the sea. Dreadful nightmares beset me. Then my brain grew calmer, my imagination wandered into pleasanter fancies, and I soon fell into a deep sleep.

How long we slept I do not know; but it must have lasted several hours, for it rested us completely from our fatigues. I woke first. My companions had not moved, and were still stretched in their corner.

Hardly roused from my somewhat hard couch, I felt my brain free, my mind clear. I again undertook a close examination of our cell. Nothing had really changed. The prison was still a prison — the prisoners, prisoners. However, the steward, during our sleep, had cleared the table.

I found that I was breathing with difficulty. The air was heavy and oppressed my lungs. Although the cell was large, we had evidently consumed a great part of the oxygen that it contained. How would the commander of this floating dwelling place get fresh air? Would he obtain it by chemical means? Or would he rise and take breath at the surface of the water, like a cetacean, and so renew for twenty-four hours the atmospheric provision?

Then I felt the boat rolling. So the iron-plated monster had evidently just risen to the surface of the ocean to breathe, after the fashion of whales. Now I knew the mode of ventilating the boat.

Above the door was a ventilator, through which volumes of fresh air quickly renewed the impoverished atmosphere of the cell.

I was making my observations, when Ned and Conseil awoke almost at the same time, under the influence of this reviving air. They rubbed their eyes, stretched themselves, and were on their feet in an instant.

"Did master sleep well?" asked Conseil, with his usual politeness.

"Very well, my brave boy. And you, Master Land?"

"Soundly, Professor. I don't know if I am right or not, but there seems to be a sea breeze!"

I told the Canadian all that had passed during his sleep, and he said next, "Professor Aronnax, I have no idea what time it is. Is it dinnertime?"

"Dinnertime! my good fellow? Say rather breakfast time, for we certainly have begun another day."

"So," said Conseil, "we have slept twenty-four hours?"

"That is my opinion," I said.

"I will not contradict you," replied Ned

Land. "But dinner or breakfast, the steward will be welcome, whichever he brings."

"Master Land, we must conform to the rules on board, and I suppose our appetites are in advance of the dining hour."

"That is just like you, friend Conseil," said Ned, impatiently. "You are never out of temper, always calm. You would die of hunger rather than complain!"

Time was getting on, and we were now fearfully hungry. And this time the steward did not appear. It was rather too long to leave us, if they really had good intentions toward us. Ned Land, tormented by the cravings of hunger, grew steadily more angry, and I dreaded an explosion when (and if) one of the crew should enter.

For two hours more Ned Land's temper increased. He cried out. He shouted, but in vain. The walls were deaf. There was no sound to be heard in the boat. All was still as death. Plunged in the depths of the waters, it belonged no longer to earth. This silence was dreadful.

I felt terrified. Conseil was calm, Ned Land roared.

Just then a noise was heard outside. Steps

sounded on metal. The locks were turned, the door opened, and the steward appeared.

Before I could rush forward to stop him, the Canadian had thrown him down, and held him by the throat. The steward was choking under the grip of his powerful hand.

Conseil was already trying to unclasp the harpooner's hand from his half-suffocated victim, and I was going to fly to the rescue, when suddenly I was nailed to the spot by hearing these words in French:

"Be quiet, Master Land. And you, Professor, will be so good as to listen to me?"

THE MAN OF THE SEAS

IT WAS THE COMMANDER of the vessel who thus spoke!

Leaning against the table, arms folded, he studied us carefully.

After some moments of silence, which not one of us dreamed of breaking, "Gentlemen," said he, in a calm and penetrating voice, "I speak French, English, German, and Latin equally well. I could, therefore, have answered you at our first interview, but I wished to know you first, then to reflect. The story told by each one, entirely agreeing in the main points, convinced me of your identity. I know now that chance has brought before me Professor Pierre Aronnax, Professor of Natural History at the Museum of Paris, entrusted with a scientific mission abroad. Also, Conseil his servant, and Ned Land, of Canadian origin, harpooner on board the frigate *Abraham Lincoln* of the navy of the United States of America."

I bowed assent. This man expressed himself with perfect ease, without any accent. His words were clear, and his fluency of speech was remarkable. Yet I did not recognize him as a fellow-countryman.

He continued the conversation.

"You have doubtless thought, sir, that I have delayed too long in paying you this second visit. The reason is that, your identity recognized, I wished to consider future plans. Most annoying circumstances have brought you into the presence of a man who has broken all the ties of humanity. You have come to trouble my existence."

"Unintentionally!" said I.

"Unintentionally?" replied the stranger, raising his voice a little. "Was it unintentionally that the *Abraham Lincoln* pursued me all over the seas? Was it unintentionally that your cannon balls rebounded off the plating of my vessel? Was it unintentionally that Master Ned Land struck me with his harpoon?"

I had a very natural answer to make and I

made it. "Sir," said I, "no doubt you are ignorant of the discussions which have taken place concerning you in America and Europe. You do not know that accidents caused by collisions with your submarine machine, have excited public feeling on two continents. You must understand that, in pursuing you over the high seas of the Pacific, the *Abraham Lincoln* believed itself to be chasing some powerful sea-monster, of which it was necessary to rid the ocean at any price."

A half smile curled the lips of the commander. Then in a calmer tone he said, "Professor, dare you say that your frigate would not as soon have pursued and cannonaded a submarine boat as a monster?"

This question embarrassed me, for I felt that Captain Farragut would not have hesitated. He would have thought it was his duty to destroy a contrivance of this kind.

"You understand then, sir," continued the stranger, "that I have the right to treat you as enemies?"

I answered nothing, for what good would discussion be, when force could destroy the best arguments?

"I have hesitated for some time," continued the commander. "Nothing obliged me to show you hospitality. If I chose to separate myself from you, I should have no interest in seeing you again. I could place you upon the deck of this vessel which has served you as a refuge, I could sink beneath the waters, and forget that you had ever existed. Would not that be my right?"

"It might be the right of a savage," I answered, "but not that of a civilized man."

"Professor," replied the commander quickly, "I am not what you call a civilized man! I have done with society entirely, for reasons which I alone have the right of appreciating. I do not therefore obey its laws, and I desire you never to allude to them before me again!"

A flash of anger and disdain kindled in his eyes, and I had a glimpse of a terrible past in the life of this man. Not only had he put himself beyond human laws, but he had made himself independent of them — free in the strictest sense of the word, quite beyond their reach. Who would dare to pursue him at the bottom of the sea, when on its surface he defied all attempts made against him? What vessel could resist the shock of his submarine?

After rather a long silence, the commander resumed the conversation. "You will remain on board my vessel, since fate has cast you there. You will be free. And in exchange for this liberty, I shall only impose one single condition. Your word of honor to submit to it will suffice."

"Speak, sir," I answered. "I suppose this condition is one which a man of honor may accept?"

"Yes, sir. It is this. It is possible that certain events, unforeseen, may oblige me to keep you to your cabins for some hours or some days, as the case may be. As I desire never to use violence, I expect from you, more than all the others, obedience. In thus acting I take all the responsibility. I acquit you entirely, for I make it an impossibility for you to see what ought not to be seen. Do you accept this condition?"

"We accept," I answered, "only I will ask your permission, sir, to address one question to you — one only."

"Speak, sir."

"You said that we should be free on board."

"Entirely."

"I ask you, then, what you mean by this liberty?"

"Just the liberty to go, to come, to see, to observe, even, all that passes here, save under rare circumstance, the liberty, in short, which we enjoy ourselves, my companions and I."

It was evident that we did not understand one another.

"Pardon me, sir," I resumed, "but this liberty is only what every prisoner has of pacing his prison. It is not enough."

"It must be however."

"What! We must give up forever seeing our country, our friends, our relations again?"

"Yes, sir. But to give up that unendurably worldly yoke which men believe to be liberty, is not perhaps so painful as you think."

"Well," exclaimed Ned Land, "never will I give my word of honor not to try to escape."

"I did not ask you for your word of honor, Master Land," answered the commander coldly.

"Sir," I replied, beginning to get angry in spite of myself, "you abuse your situation toward us. It is cruelty."

"No, sir, it is clemency. You are my prisoners of war. I keep you, when I could, by a word, plunge you into the depths of the ocean. You attacked me. You came to surprise a secret which no man in the world must penetrate — the secret of my whole existence. And you think that I am going to send you back to that world which must know me no more? Never!"

"So, sir," I answered, "you give us simply the choice between life and death?"

"Simply."

"My friends," said I, "to a question thus put, there is nothing to answer. But no word of honor binds us to the master of this vessel."

"None, sir," answered the Unknown.

Then, in a gentler tone, he continued:

"Now permit me to finish what I have to say to you. I know you, Professor Aronnax. You and your companions will not perhaps, have so much to complain of in the chance which has bound you to my fate. You will find among the books which are my favorite study the work which you have published on the depths of the sea. I have often read it. You have carried your work as far as terrestrial science permitted you. But you do not know all — you have not seen all. Let me tell you then, Professor, that you will not regret the time passed on board my vessel. You are going to visit the land of marvels."

These words of the commander had a great effect upon me. I cannot deny it. My weak point was touched.

"By what name ought I to address you?" I asked.

"Sir," replied the commander, "I am nothing to you but Captain Nemo, and you and your companions are nothing to me but the passengers of the *Nautilus*."

Captain Nemo called. A steward appeared. The captain gave him his orders in that strange language which I did not understand. Then, turning toward the Canadian and Conseil he said, "A repast awaits you in your cabin. Be so good as to follow this man. And now, Professor, our breakfast is ready. Permit me to lead the way."

I followed Captain Nemo, and as soon as I had passed through the door, I found myself in a kind of passage lighted by electricity. After we had proceeded a dozen yards, a second door opened before me.

I then entered a dining room, decorated and furnished in severe taste. High oaken sideboards, inlaid with ebony, stood at the two extremities of the room, and upon their shelves glittered china, porcelain, and glass of inestimable value. The silver on the table sparkled in the rays which the luminous ceiling shed around, while the light was tempered and softened by exquisite paintings.

In the center of the room was a table richly laid out. Captain Nemo indicated the place I was to occupy.

The breakfast consisted of a certain number of dishes, the contents of which I soon found out were furnished by the sea alone. I was ignorant of some of them. I acknowledged that they were good, but they had a peculiar flavor, but I easily became accustomed to it. I guessed at once that they must have a marine origin.

Captain Nemo looked at me. I asked him no questions, but he guessed my thoughts, and answered of his own accord the questions which I was burning to address to him.

"The greater part of these dishes are unknown to you," he said to me. "However, they are wholesome and nourishing. For a long time I have renounced the food of the earth, and am never ill now. My crew, who are healthy, are fed on the same food."

"So," said I, "all these eatables are the produce of the sea?"

"Yes, Professor, the sea supplies all my wants. Sometimes I cast my nets in tow, and I draw them in filled to breaking. Sometimes I hunt in the midst of this element, which appears to be inaccessible to man, and quarry the game which dwells in my submarine forests."

"I can understand perfectly, sir, that your nets furnish excellent fish for your table. I can understand also that you hunt aquatic game in your submarine forests. But I cannot understand at all how meat can figure in your bill of fare."

"This, which you believe to be meat, Professor, is nothing else than filet of turtle. Here are also some dolphins' livers, which you take to be pork. My cook is a clever fellow, who excels in dressing these various products of the ocean. Taste all these dishes."

I tasted more while Captain Nemo enchanted me with his extraordinary stories.

"You like the sea, Captain?"

"Yes, I love it! The sea is everything. It covers seven-tenths of the globe. Its breath is pure and healthy. It is an immense desert, where man is never lonely, for he feels life stirring on all sides. In fact, Professor, Nature manifests herself in it by her three kingdoms, mineral, vegetable, and animal. The sea is the vast reservoir of Nature. The earth began with sea, so to speak. And who knows if it will not end with it? Upon its surface men can still exercise unjust laws, fight, tear one another to pieces. But at thirty feet below its level, their reign ceases, their influence is quenched, and their power disappears. Ah! sir, live — live in the bosom of the waters!

There only is independence! There I recognize no masters! There I am free!"

Captain Nemo suddenly became silent in the midst of his enthusiasm, although he had been quite carried away. For a few moments he paced up and down, much agitated. Then he became more calm, regained his accustomed coldness of expression, and turning toward me:

"Now, Professor," said he, "if you wish to go over the *Nautilus*, I am at your service."

Captain Nemo rose. I followed him. A double door at the back of the dining room opened. I entered a room equal in dimensions to that which I had just quitted.

It was a library. High pieces of furniture, of black violet ebony inland with brass, supported upon their wide shelves a great number of books. Electric light flooded everything. I looked with real admiration at this room, so ingeniously fitted up, and I could scarcely believe my eyes.

"Captain Nemo," said I, "this is a library which would do honor to a palace. I am absolutely astounded when I consider that it can follow you to the bottom of the seas."

"Where could one find greater solitude or silence, Professor?" replied Captain Nemo.

"Did your study in the museum afford you such perfect quiet?"

"No, sir; and I must confess that it is a very poor one after yours. You must have six or seven thousand volumes here."

"Twelve thousand, Professor Aronnax. These are the only ties which bind me to the earth. But I had done with the world on the day when my *Nautilus* plunged for the first time beneath the waters. That day I bought my last volumes, my last pamphlets, my last papers, and from that time I wish to think that men no longer think or write. These books, Professor, are at your service, and you can make use of them freely."

Then Captain Nemo opened a door which stood opposite to that by which I had entered the library and I passed into an immense drawing room splendidly lighted.

It was a vast four-sided room, thirty feet long, eighteen wide, and fifteen high. A luminous ceiling shed a soft clear light over all the marvels in this museum. For it was in fact a museum.

Thirty first-rate pictures, uniformly framed, ornamented the walls, which were hung with tapestry of severe design. I saw works of great value, the greater part of which

I had admired in the special collections and exhibitions in Europe.

"Sir," I said, "without seeking to know who you are, I recognize in you an artist."

"An amateur, nothing more, sir. Formerly, I loved to collect these beautiful works created by the hand of man. I sought them greedily, and I have been able to bring together some objects of great value. These are my last souvenirs of that world which is dead to me." Captain Nemo pointed to some music scattered over a large piano-organ which occupied one of the panels of the drawing room.

Then he was silent. Leaning on his elbow against an angle of a costly mosaic table, he no longer saw me — he had forgotten my presence.

I continued my observation of the curiosities which enriched this drawing room.

Under elegant glass cases, fixed by copper rivets, were classed and labeled the most precious treasures of the sea ever presented to the eye of a naturalist — or any man.

An infinite variety of the sea's produce were carefully displayed in their separate categories — sponges, corals, mollusks, and rare shells from Australian waters, the Gulf of Mexico, the Indian Ocean and Norwegian waters. Apart, in separate compartments, were spread out chaplets of pearls of the greatest beauty, which reflected the electric light in little sparks of fire; pink pearls, torn from the pinna-marina of the Red Sea; green pearls, yellow, blue and black pearls — those curious productions of the mollusks of every ocean and of certain mussels of Northern waters; and, most striking, were several specimens of pearls — larger than a pigeon's egg!

"You are examining my collection, Professor?" Captain Nemo asked. "Unquestionably they must be interesting to a naturalist. But for me they have a far greater charm, for I have collected them all with my own hand, and there is not a sea on the face of the globe which has escaped my researches."

"I can understand, Captain, the delight of wandering about in the midst of such riches," I answered. "You are one of those who have collected their treasures themselves. No museum in Europe possesses such a collection of the produce of the ocean. I must confess that this *Nautilus* excites my curiosity to the highest pitch. I see suspended on the walls of this room instruments of whose use I am ignorant."

"You will find these same instruments in my own room, Professor, where I shall have much pleasure in explaining their use to you. But first, come and inspect the cabin which is set apart for your own use. You must see how you will be accommodated on board the *Nautilus*."

I followed Captain Nemo, who conducted me toward the bow, and there I found, not a cabin, but an elegant room with a bed, dressing table and several other pieces of furniture.

I could only thank my host.

"Your room adjoins mine," said he, opening a door, "and mine opens into the drawing room that we have just quitted."

I entered the captain's room. It had a severe, almost monkish aspect. A small iron bedstead, a table and some articles for the toilet — the whole lighted by a skylight. No comforts — the strictest necessaries only.

Captain Nemo pointed to a seat. "Be so good as to sit down," he said. I seated myself, and he began. . . .

ALL BY ELECTRICITY

"SIR," said Captain Nemo, showing me the instruments hanging on the walls of his room, "here are the contrivances required for the navigation of the *Nautilus*. Here, as in the drawing room, I have them always under my eyes, and they indicate my position and exact direction in the middle of the ocean. Some are known to you, such as the thermometer, which gives the internal temperature of the *Nautilus*. The barometer indicates the weight of the air and foretells the changes of the weather. The hygrometer marks the dryness of the atmosphere. The storm-glass, the contents of which, by decomposing, announces the approach of storms. The compass guides my course. The sextant shows the latitude by the altitude of the sun. And by chronometers I calculate the longitude. And I have spyglasses for day and night, which I use to examine the points of the horizon, when the *Nautilus* rises to the surface of the waves."

"These are the usual nautical instruments," I replied, "and I know the use of them. But these others, no doubt, answer to the particular requirements of the *Nautilus*. This dial with the movable needle is a manometer, is it not?"

"It is, and by contact with the water, whose external pressure it indicates, it gives our depth at the same time."

"And these other instruments, the use of which I cannot guess?"

He was silent for a few moments, then he said, "There is a powerful agent, obedient, rapid, easy, which conforms to every use, and reigns supreme on board my vessel. Everything is done by means of it. It lights it, warms it, and is the soul of my mechanical apparatus. This agent is electricity."

"Electricity?" I cried in surprise.

"Yes, sir," he replied. "Electricity gives heat, light, motion, and, in a word, life to the *Nautilus*."

"But not the air you breathe?"

"Oh! I could manufacture the air necessary, but it is needless, because I go up to the surface of the water when I please. However, electricity does operate the powerful pumps which store air in large tanks. These enable me to prolong my stay in the depths of the sea. And electricity gives constant light, which the sun does not. Now look at this clock; it too is electrical, and goes with a regularity that defies the best chronometers. It tells time over a period of twenty-four hours. For me there is neither night nor day, sun or moon, but only that light that I take with me to the bottom of the sea. Look! Just now, it is ten o'clock in the morning."

"Exactly."

"Another application of electricity. This dial hanging in front of us indicates the speed of the *Nautilus*. An electric wire connects with the screw propeller, and the needle indicates the real speed. Look! Now we are cruising along at 15 knots."

"It is marvelous! And I see, Captain, you were right to make use of this agent that takes the place of wind, water, and steam."

"We have not finished," said Captain Nemo, rising. "If you will follow me, we will go to the stern of the *Nautilus*."

I knew already the forward part of this sub-

72

marine boat. The exact division, starting from the ship's prow, was first the dining room, 15 feet long, separated from the library by a watertight partition; the library, 15 feet long; the large drawing room, 30 feet long, separated from the captain's room by a second watertight partition. His room was 15 feet in length. Mine was $7\frac{1}{2}$ feet. Lastly, a tank of air, $22\frac{1}{2}$ feet long, extended to the bows. Total length, 35 yards, or 105 feet. The partitions had doors that were shut hermetically by a rubber seal. They ensured the safety of the *Nautilus* in case of a leak.

Now I followed Captain Nemo to the center of the boat. There, an iron ladder was fastened by an iron hook to the partition. I asked the captain what the ladder was used for.

"It leads to the small boat," he said.

"What! Have you a boat?" I exclaimed, in surprise.

"Of course. An excellent vessel, light and unsinkable, that serves either as a fishing or as a pleasure boat."

"But then, when you wish to embark, you are obliged to come to the surface of the water?"

"Not at all. This boat is stored in the upper part of the hull of the *Nautilus*. It is decked, quite watertight, and held together by solid bolts. This ladder leads to a manhole made in the hull of the *Nautilus*, that corresponds with a similar hole made in the side of the boat. By this double opening I get into the small vessel. The crew shuts one and I shut the other. Then I undo the bolts, and the little boat goes up to the surface of the sea with great rapidity. I then open the panel of the bridge, carefully shut till then. I mast it, hoist my sail, take my oars, and I'm off."

"But how do you get back on board?"

"I do not come back, Professor. The *Nautilus* comes to me, by my orders. An electric wire connects us. I telegraph to it, and that is enough."

"Really!" I said, astonished at these marvels.

After having passed by the cage of the staircase that led to the platform, was a cabin 6 feet long, where Conseil and Ned Land were having breakfast. Beyond, a door opened into a kitchen 9 feet long, situated between the large storerooms. There electricity did all the cooking. Near this kitchen was a bathroom comfortably furnished, with hot and cold water taps.

Next to the kitchen was the berthroom of the vessel, 16 feet long. But the door was shut, and I could not see the management of it, which might have given me an idea of the number of men employed on board the *Nautilus*.

A fourth partition led to the engine room. This engine room, clearly lighted, did not measure less than 65 feet in length. It was divided into two parts. The first contained the materials for producing electricity, and the second the machinery that connected it with the propeller. I examined it all with great interest.

"Ah, Commander!" I said, "your *Nautilus* is certainly a marvelous boat."

"Yes, Professor, and I love it as if it were part of myself. On the *Nautilus* men's hearts never fail them. There are no defects to be afraid of, for the double shell is as firm as iron; no fire to fear, for the vessel is made of iron; no coal supplies to run short, for the electricity is otherwise powered as you will understand later. And there is no tempest to brave, for when the boat dives below the water it reaches absolute tranquillity. There, sir! that is the perfection of vessels! And, you understand the trust I repose in my *Nautilus* — for I am at once captain, builder, and engineer."

"But how could you construct this wonderful *Nautilus* in secret?" I asked.

"Each separate portion was brought from

different parts of the globe, and each part was ordered by me under different names."

"But these parts had to be put together and arranged?"

"Professor, I had set up my workshops upon a desert island in the ocean. There my workmen, that is to say, the brave men that I instructed and educated, and myself have put together our *Nautilus*. Then when the work was finished, fire destroyed all trace of our proceedings on this island."

"One last question, Captain Nemo."

"Ask it, Professor."

"You are rich?"

"Immensely rich, sir; and I could, without missing it, pay the national debt of France!"

"Sir," said Captain Nemo, "we will now take our bearings and fix the starting point of this voyage. It is a quarter to twelve. I will go up to the surface."

The captain pressed an electric clock three times. The pumps began to drive the water from the tanks. The needle of the manometer marked by a different pressure the ascent of the *Nautilus*, then it stopped.

"We have arrived," said the captain.

I went to the central staircase which opened

on to the platform, clambered up the iron steps, and found myself on the upper part of the *Nautilus*.

The platform was only three feet out of water. The spindle-shaped ends of the *Nautilus* could be compared to a cigar. I noticed that its iron plates, slightly overlaying each other, resembled the shell which clothes the bodies of our large land reptiles. It was not surprising that this boat should have been taken for a marine animal.

Toward the middle of the platform the small boat, half buried in the hull of the vessel, formed a slight curve. Fore and aft rose two cages of medium height with inclined glass-enclosed sides. One side was for the steersman who directed the *Nautilus*, the other contained a brilliant lantern to give light on the road.

The sea was beautiful, the sky pure. A light breeze from the east rippled the surface of the waters. The horizon, free from fog, made observation easy. Nothing was in sight — not an island.

Captain Nemo, by the help of his sextant, took the altitude of the sun, which ought also to give the latitude. He waited for some moments till its disc touched the horizon. While taking observations not a muscle moved, the instrument could not have been more motionless in a hand of marble.

"Twelve o'clock, sir," said he. "Shall we go below?"

I cast a look upon the sea, slightly yellowed by the Japanese coast, and descended to the salon.

"And now, sir, I leave you to your studies," added the captain; "our course is E.N.E., our depth will be 26 fathoms. Here are maps on a large scale by which you may follow it. The salon is at your disposal, and with your permission I will retire." Captain Nemo bowed, and I remained alone, lost in thoughts all bearing on the commander of the *Nautilus*.

For a whole hour was I deep in these reflections, seeking to pierce this mystery so interesting to me. Then my eyes fell upon the vast planisphere spread upon the table, and I placed my finger on the very spot where the given latitude and longitude crossed.

Ned Land and Conseil then appeared at the door of the salon.

My two brave companions were astonished by the wonders spread before them.

"Where are we, where are we?" exclaimed the Canadian. "In the museum at Quebec?"

"My friends," I answered, making a sign for

them to enter, "you are not in Canada, but on board the *Nautilus* 50 yards below the level of the sea."

"Professor," said Ned Land, "have you learned how many men there are on board? Ten, twenty, fifty, a hundred?"

"I cannot answer you, Mr. Land. It is better to abandon for a time all idea of seizing the *Nautilus* or escaping from it. This ship is a masterpiece of modern industry, and I should be sorry not to have seen it. Many people would accept the situation forced upon us, if only to move among such wonders. So be quiet and let us try and see what passes around us."

"*See!*" exclaimed the harpooner, "but we can see nothing in this iron prison! We are walking — we are sailing — blindly."

Ned Land had scarcely pronounced these words when all was suddenly darkness. The luminous ceiling was gone, and so rapidly that my eyes received a painful impression.

We remained mute, not stirring, and not knowing what surprise awaited us, whether agreeable or disagreeable. A sliding noise was heard. One would have said that panels were working at the sides of the *Nautilus*.

"It is the end of the end!" said Ned Land.

Suddenly light broke at each side of the

salon, through two openings. The water was vividly lighted by the electric gleam. Two crystal plates separated us from the sea. At first I trembled at the thought that this frail partition might break, but strong bands of copper bound them, giving an almost infinite power of resistance.

The sea was distinctly visible for a mile all round the *Nautilus*. What a spectacle! Who could paint the effects of the light through those transparent sheets of water?

On each side a window opened into this unexplored abyss. The darkness of the salon showed to advantage the brightness outside, and we looked out as if this pure crystal had been the glass of an immense aquarium.

"You wished to see, friend Ned — well, you see now."

"Curious! curious!" muttered the Canadian, forgetting his ill-temper. "And one would come farther than this to admire such a sight!"

For two whole hours an aquatic army escorted the *Nautilus*, and our imagination was kept at its height. Ned named the fish, and Conseil classed them. Never had it been given to me to see these animals, alive and at liberty, in their natural element. I will not mention all the varieties which passed before my dazzled eyes, all the collection of the seas of China and Japan. These fish, more numerous than the birds of the air, came, attracted, no doubt, by the brilliant focus of the electric light.

Suddenly there was daylight in the salon, the panels closed again, and the enchanting vision disappeared. But for a long time I dreamed on till my eyes fell on the instruments hanging on the partition. The compass still showed the course to be E.N.E. The manometer indicated a pressure of five atmospheres, equivalent to a depth of 25 fathoms, and the electric log gave a speed of 15 miles an hour. I expected Captain Nemo, but he did not appear. The clock marked the hour of five.

Ned Land and Conseil returned to their cabin, and I retired to my chamber. My dinner was ready.

I passed the evening reading, writing, and thinking. Then sleep overpowered me, and I stretched myself on my couch and slept profoundly.

A NOTE OF INVITATION

THE NEXT DAY was the 9th of November. I awoke after a long sleep of twelve hours. As soon as I was dressed I went into the salon. It was deserted.

I plunged into the study of the shell treasures and also the rarest marine plants, which, although dried up, retained their lovely colors.

The whole day passed without a visit from Captain Nemo. The panels of the salon did not open. Perhaps he did not wish us to tire of the beautiful underwater view.

The next day, 10th of November, was the same. Ned and Conseil spent the greater part of the day with me. They were astonished at the absence of the captain. Was this strange man ill? Had he softened in his attitude toward us?

After all, as Conseil said, we enjoyed perfect liberty, and we were delicately and abundantly fed. We could not complain.

That day I commenced the journal of these adventures which has enabled me to relate them in detail. I wrote it on paper made from the zostera marina.

On the 11th of November, early in the morning, the fresh air spreading over the interior of the *Nautilus* told me that we had come to the surface of the ocean to renew our supply of oxygen. I went to the central staircase, and mounted the platform.

It was six o'clock, the weather was cloudy, the sea gray but calm — scarcely a billow. Would Captain Nemo, whom I hoped to meet, be there? I saw no one but the steersman in his glass cage. Seated upon the projection formed by the hull of the long boat, I inhaled the salt breeze with delight.

By degrees, the fog disappeared under the action of the sun's rays as the radiant orb rose in the sky. The sea flamed under its glare. The clouds were colored with lively tints, and numerous "mare's tails" betokened wind for that day. But what was wind to this *Nautilus* which tempests could not frighten!

I was admiring this joyous rising of the sun, so gay, and so lifegiving, when I heard steps approaching the platform. I was prepared to salute Captain Nemo, but it was his second officer who appeared. He advanced on the platform, not seeming to see me. With his powerful spyglass he scanned every point of the horizon with great attention. This over, he approached the panel and pronounced a sentence in exactly these strange words (I have remembered it, for every morning it was repeated under exactly the same conditions):

"Nautron respoc lorni virch."

These words pronounced, the officer descended. I thought that the *Nautilus* was about to return to its submarine navigation, so I returned to my chamber.

Five days sped thus, without any change in our situation. Every morning I mounted the platform. The same phrase was pronounced by the same individual. But Captain Nemo did not appear.

I had made up my mind that I should never see him again, when, on the 16th of November, on returning to my room with Ned and Conseil, I found on my table this note, written in a bold, clear hand:

16th of November, 1867

TO PROFESSOR ARONNAX, on board the *Nautilus:*
Captain Nemo invites Professor Aronnax to a hunting party, which will take place tomorrow morning in the forests of the island of Crespo. He hopes that nothing will prevent the Professor from being present, and he will with pleasure see him joined by his companions.

CAPTAIN NEMO,
Commander of the *Nautilus.*

"A hunt on land!" exclaimed Ned. "I shall not be sorry to eat a piece of fresh venison."

"Let us first see where the island of Crespo is."

I consulted the planisphere, and in 32° 40′ N. lat., and 157° 50′ W. long., I found a small island, discovered in 1801 by Captain Crespo, and marked in the ancient Spanish maps as Rocca de la Plata, the meaning of which is "The Silver Rock." I also noted that we were then about 1800 miles from our starting point, and that the course of the *Nautilus*, a little changed, was bringing it back toward the southeast.

I showed this little rock lost in the midst of the North Pacific to my companions.

"If Captain Nemo does sometimes go on dry ground," said I, "he chooses desert islands."

Ned Land shrugged his shoulders without speaking, and he and Conseil left me.

The next morning, on awakening, I could feel that the *Nautilus* was perfectly still. I dressed quickly and entered the salon.

Captain Nemo was there, waiting for me. He rose, bowed, and asked me to accompany him. I did not mention his absence of the last eight days, and simply answered that I and my companions were ready to follow him.

We entered the dining room, where breakfast was served.

"Professor," said the captain, "pray share my breakfast; we will chat as we eat. For though I promised you a walk in the forest, I did not promise to find hotels there. So breakfast as a man who will most likely not have his dinner until very late."

I did honor to the repast. It was composed of several kinds of fish, and different sorts of seaweed.

Captain Nemo ate silently at first. Then:

"Sir, when I told you that I proposed to hunt in my *submarine* forest of Crespo, you evidently thought me mad, but you know as I do, Professor, that man can live under water, if he carries with him a sufficient supply of breathable air. In submarine work, the workman, clad in waterproof gear with his head in a metal helmet, receives air from above by means of forcing pumps and regulators. But under these conditions the man is not at liberty. He is attached to the pump by the breathing tube. If we are obliged to be thus held to the *Nautilus*, we could not go far."

"And the means of getting free?" I asked.

"It is to use the Rouquayrol apparatus, invented by two of your own countrymen, which I have brought to perfection for my own use. It consists of an air tank of thick iron plates, in which I store the air under pressure. This tank is fixed on the back by means of braces, like a soldier's knapsack. Its upper part forms a box in which the air is kept by means of a bellows, and therefore cannot escape unless at its normal pressure. In the apparatus such as we use, two rubber tubes from this box join a sort of tent over the nose and mouth. One tube is to introduce fresh air, the other to let out the foul, and the tongue closes one or the other according to the wants of the breather. But in encountering great pressures at the bottom of the sea, I enclose my head, like a diver, in a ball of copper; and it is into this ball of copper that the two pipes lead. The tank apparatus can furnish breathable air for nine or ten hours."

"Captain," I asked, "how can you light your way at the bottom of the sea?"

"With the Ruhmkorff apparatus, Professor. When the apparatus is at work luminous gas gives out a white and continuous light. Thus provided, I can breathe and I can see."

"And as to the gun I am to carry?" I asked.

"It is not a gun for powder," answered the captain.

"Then it is an air-gun."

"Doubtless! How would you have me manufacture gunpowder on board, without either saltpeter, sulphur or charcoal?"

"Besides," I added, "to fire under water in a medium eight hundred and fifty-five times denser than the air, we must conquer very considerable resistance. It seems to me that in this twilight, and in the midst of this fluid, which is very dense compared with the atmosphere, shots could not go far, nor easily prove mortal."

"Sir, on the contrary, with this gun every blow is mortal; and however lightly the animal is touched, it falls as if struck by a thunderbolt."

"Why?"

"Because the balls sent by this gun are glass cases covered with a case of steel, and weighted with a pellet of lead, and into which the electricity is forced to a very high tension. With the slightest shock they are discharged, and the animal, however strong it may be, falls dead. I must tell you that these cases are size number four, and that the charge for an ordinary gun would be ten."

"I will say no more," I replied, rising from the table, "I will go where you go."

Captain Nemo then led me aft, and in passing before Conseil's cabin, I called my two companions, who followed immediately. We then came to a kind of cell near the machinery room, in which we were to put on our underwater gear.

A WALK ON THE BOTTOM OF THE SEA

THIS CELL was, to speak correctly, the arsenal and wardrobe of the *Nautilus*. A dozen diving apparatuses hung from the partition, waiting our use. Ned Land, on seeing them, showed reluctance to put one on. "But, my worthy Ned, the forests of the island of Crespo are submarine forests."

The disappointed harpooner saw his dreams of fresh meat fade away. "And you, Professor, are you going to dress yourself in those clothes?"

"There is no alternative, Master Ned."

"As you please, sir," replied the harpooner, shrugging his shoulders. "But as for me, unless I am forced, I will never get into one."

"No one will force you, Master Ned," said Captain Nemo.

"Is Conseil going to risk it?" asked Ned.

"I follow my master wherever he goes," replied Conseil.

At the captain's call two of the ship's crew came to help us to dress in these heavy waterproof clothes, made of seamless rubber and constructed to resist considerable pressure. The suit was both supple and resisting. We wore thick boots, weighted with heavy leaden soles.

Bands of copper crossed the upper part of the suit, protecting the chest from the great pressure of the water, and leaving the lungs free to act. The sleeves ended in gloves, which in no way restrained the movement of the hands.

Captain Nemo and one of his companions — a sort of Hercules, who must have possessed great strength — Conseil, and myself, were soon dressed. Nothing remained to do but enclose our heads in the metal balls. But before this, I asked the captain's permission to examine the guns we were to carry.

One of the *Nautilus* men gave me a simple gun, the butt end of which, made of steel, hollow in the center, was rather large. It served as a tank for compressed air, which a valve, worked by a spring, allowed to escape into a metal tube. A box of projectiles, in a groove in the thickness of the butt end, contained about twenty of the balls previously described, which, by means of a spring, were forced into the barrel of the gun. As soon as one shot was fired, another was ready.

"Captain Nemo," said I, "this gun is perfect, and easily handled — I only ask to be allowed to try it. But how shall we reach the bottom of the sea?"

"At this moment, Professor, the *Nautilus* is at five fathoms, and we have nothing to do but to start."

"But how shall we get off?"

"You shall see."

Captain Nemo thrust his head into the helmet, Conseil and I did the same, not without hearing an ironical "Good sport!" from the Canadian. The upper part of our dress terminated in a copper collar, upon which was screwed the metal helmet. Three holes, protected by thick glass, allowed us to see in several directions. As soon as the helmet was in position, the breathing apparatus on our backs began to act, and for my part, I could breathe with ease.

With the lamp hanging from my belt, and the gun in my hand, I was ready. But im-

prisoned in these heavy garments, and glued
to the deck by my leaden soles, I found it was
impossible for me to take a step.

Then I felt myself being pushed ahead into
a little room. My companions followed, pushed
along in the same way. I heard a watertight
door, furnished with stopper plates, close upon
us, and we were wrapped in profound darkness.

After some minutes, a loud hissing was
heard. I felt the cold mount my feet to my
chest. Evidently from some part of the vessel
they had, by means of a tap, given entrance
to the water, and the room was soon filled. A
second door cut in the side of the *Nautilus*
then opened. We saw a faint light. In another
instant our feet trod the bottom of the sea.

And now, how can I retrace the impression
left upon me by that walk under the waters?
Words cannot relate such wonders! Captain
Nemo walked in front, his companion followed
some steps behind. Conseil and I remained
near each other. I no longer felt the weight of
my clothing, or of my shoes, of my air tank,
or my thick helmet.

The light, which lit the bottom 30 feet below the surface of the ocean, astonished me
by its power. The solar rays shone through
the watery mass easily, and dissipated all

color, and I clearly distinguished objects at a distance of 150 yards. Beyond that the tints darkened into fine gradations of ultramarine, and faded into vague obscurity. Truly this water which surrounded me was but another air denser than the terrestrial atmosphere, but almost as transparent. Above me was the calm surface of the sea.

We were walking on fine even sand, not wrinkled, as on a flat shore, which retains the impression of the billows. This dazzling carpet was a reflector of the sun's rays. Shall I be believed when I say that, at the depth of 30 feet, I could see as if I was in broad daylight?

For a quarter of an hour I trod on this sand. The hull of the *Nautilus*, resembling a long shoal, disappeared by degrees. But its lantern, when darkness should overtake us in the waters, would help to guide us on board by its distinct rays.

It was then ten in the morning. The rays of the sun struck the surface of the waves, and flowers, rocks, plants, shells, and polypi were shaded in a perfect kaleidoscope of green, yellow, orange, violet, indigo, and blue. I tried to communicate to Conseil by signs the lively sensations which were mounting to my brain.

Various kinds of isis, clusters of pure tuft-coral, prickly fungi, and anemones, formed a brilliant garden of flowers. It was a real grief to me to crush under my feet the brilliant specimens of mollusks which strewed the ground by thousands — red helmet-shells, angel-wings, and many others produced by this inexhaustible ocean.

All these wonders I saw in the space of a quarter of a mile, scarcely stopping, and following Captain Nemo, who beckoned me on. Soon the nature of the bottom changed to slimy mud. We then traveled over a seaweed plain of wild and luxuriant vegetation. This was of close texture, and soft to the feet, and rivaled the softest carpet woven by man. A light network of marine plants, of that inexhaustible family of seaweeds — of which more than 2000 kinds are known — grew on the surface of the water. From them I saw long floating ribbons hanging, some globular, others tuberous, and I saw most delicate foliage resembling the fan of a cactus. I noticed that the green plants kept nearer the top of the sea, the red at a greater depth, and the black or brown formed gardens in the deepest beds of the ocean.

We had been gone from the *Nautilus* about an hour and a half. I knew by the perpendicularity of the sun's rays that it was near noon.

Now the ocean floor sloped downward and the light took a uniform tint. We were at a depth of 125 yards and 20 inches, undergoing a pressure of six atmospheres.

At this depth I could still see the rays of the sun, though feebly. Intense brilliancy faded to a reddish twilight, but we could still see well enough; it was not necessary to resort to the lamps as yet. At this moment Captain Nemo stopped. He waited till I joined him, and then pointed to a dark area looming in the shadow, at a short distance.

"It is the forest of the island of Crespo," thought I. And I was not mistaken.

A SUBMARINE FOREST

WE HAD AT LAST arrived on the borders of this forest, doubtless one of the finest of Captain Nemo's immense domains. He looked upon it as his own, and considered he had the same right over it that the first men had in the first days of the world.

This forest was composed of large tree-plants, and the moment we penetrated under its vast arcades, I was struck by the unusual position of their branches.

Not an herb which carpeted the ground, not a branch which clothed the trees, was either broken or bent, nor did they extend horizontally — all stretched up to the surface of the ocean. Not a filament, not a ribbon, however it might be, but kept as straight as a rod of iron due to the density of the element which produced them. Motionless, yet when bent to one side by the hand, they directly resumed their former position. Truly it was the region of perpendicularity!

I soon accustomed myself to the comparative darkness which surrounded us. The soil of the forest seemed covered with sharp blocks, difficult to avoid. The submarine flora struck me as being perfect. But for some minutes I mistook zoophytes for hydrophytes, animals for plants. And who would not have been mistaken? The fauna and the flora are too closely allied in this submarine world.

These plants are self-propagated, and the principle of their existence is in the water, which upholds and nourishes them. The greater number, instead of leaves, shot forth blades of many shapes — pink, carmine, green, olive, fawn, and brown. I saw numbers of other marine plants, all devoid of flowers!

"Curious, fantastic element!" said one naturalist, "in which the animal kingdom blossoms, and the vegetable does not!"

Under these numerous shrubs — as large as trees of the temperate zone — and under their damp shadow, were massed real bushes of living flowers.

In about an hour Captain Nemo gave the signal to halt. I, for my part, was not sorry, and we stretched ourselves under an arbor of long thin blades which stood up like arrows.

This short rest seemed delicious to me. There was nothing wanting but the charm of conversation. But, impossible to speak, I only put my greater copper head to Conseil's. I saw the worthy fellow's eyes glistening with delight, and to show his satisfaction, he shook himself in his breastplate of air in the most comical way in the world.

After four hours of this walking I was surprised not to find myself dreadfully hungry. Instead I felt the desire to sleep, which happens to all divers. And my eyes soon closed behind the thick glasses, and I fell into a heavy slumber, which the movement alone had prevented before.

How long I remained buried in this drowsiness I cannot judge, but when I woke, the sun seemed sinking toward the horizon. Captain Nemo had already risen, and I was beginning to stretch my limbs, when an unexpected apparition brought me briskly to my feet.

A few steps off a monstrous sea spider, about 38 inches high, was watching me with squinting eyes, ready to spring upon me. Though my diver's dress was thick enough to defend me from the bite of this animal, I could not help shuddering with horror. Conseil and the sailor of the *Nautilus* awoke at this moment. Captain Nemo pointed out the hideous crustacean, which a blow from the butt end of the gun knocked over, and I saw the horrible claws of the monster writhe in terrible convulsions. This accident reminded me that other animals more to be feared might haunt these obscure depths, against whose attacks my diving suit would not protect me.

I had never thought of it before, but I now resolved to be upon my guard. Indeed, I thought that this halt would mark the end of our walk. But I was mistaken, for, instead of returning to the *Nautilus*, Captain Nemo continued his bold excursion, leading us to greater depths. It must have been about three o'clock when we reached a narrow valley, between high perpendicular walls, about 75 fathoms deep — thanks to the perfection of our air tanks.

I say 75 fathoms, though I had no instrument by which to judge the distance. But I knew that even in the clearest waters the solar rays could not penetrate further. And accordingly the darkness deepened. At ten paces not an object was visible. I was groping my way, when I suddenly saw a brilliant white light. Captain Nemo had just put his electric lamp into use. His companion did the same, and Conseil and I followed their example. By turning a screw I established a communication between the wire and the spiral glass, and the sea, lit by our four lanterns, was illuminated for a circle of 36 yards.

Captain Nemo was still plunging into the dark depths of the forest, whose trees were getting scarcer at every step. I noticed that vegetable life disappeared sooner than animal life.

As we walked, I thought the light of our lamps could not fail to draw some inhabitant from its dark couch. But if they did approach us, they at least kept at a respectful distance. Several times I saw Captain Nemo stop, put his gun to his shoulder, and after some moments lower it and walk on. At last, after about four hours, this marvelous excursion came to an end. A steep wall of superb rocks rose before us — a heap of gigantic blocks. It was the base of the island of Crespo. It was land! Captain Nemo stopped suddenly. A gesture of his brought us all to a halt, and however desirous I might be to scale the wall, I was obliged to stop. Here ended Captain Nemo's domains. And he would not go beyond them. Farther on was a portion of the globe he would not trample upon.

The return began. Captain Nemo had returned to the head of his little band, directing their course without hesitation. I thought we were not following the same road to return to the *Nautilus*. The new road was very steep, and consequently very painful. We approached the surface of the sea rapidly. But this return to the upper strata was not so sudden as to change the pressure too rapidly. That might have produced the serious internal injuries so fatal to divers. Very soon light reappeared and grew, and the sun being low on the horizon, the refraction edged the different objects with a spectral ring. At ten yards and a half deep, we walked in a shoal of little fishes of all kinds, more numerous than the birds of the air, and also more agile. But no aquatic game worthy of a shot had as yet met our gaze, when at that moment I saw the captain shoulder his gun quickly, and follow a moving object into the shrubs. He fired. I heard a slight hissing, and a creature fell stunned at some distance from us. It was a magnificent sea otter, an enhydrus, the only exclusively marine quadruped. This otter was five feet long, and must have been very valuable. Its skin, chestnut-brown above, and silvery underneath, would have made one of those beautiful furs so sought after in the Russian and Chinese markets.

I admired this curious mammal, with its rounded head ornamented with short ears, its round eyes and white whiskers like those of a cat, with webbed feet and nails, and tufted tail. This precious animal, hunted and tracked by fishermen, has now become very rare, and taken refuge chiefly in the northern parts of the Pacific, or probably its race would have become extinct.

Captain Nemo's companion took the beast, threw it over his shoulder, and we continued our journey. For two hours we followed these sandy plains, then fields of algae very disagreeable to cross. Candidly, I felt I could go no farther when I saw a glimmer of light, which, for a half mile, broke the darkness of the waters. It was the lantern of the *Nautilus*. Before twenty minutes were over we should be on board, and I should be able to breathe with ease, for it seemed that my air tank supplied little oxygen now. But I did not reckon on an accidental meeting, which delayed our arrival for some time.

I had remained some steps behind, when I presently saw Captain Nemo coming hurriedly toward me. With his strong hand he pushed me to the ground, his companion doing the same to Conseil. At first I knew not what to think, but I was soon reassured by seeing the captain lie down beside me, and remain immovable.

I was stretched on the ground, just under

103

shelter of a bush of algae, when, raising my head, I saw some enormous mass, casting phosphorescent gleams, pass by.

My blood froze as I recognized two formidable sharks which threatened us — terrible creatures, with enormous tails and a dull glassy stare. I noticed their silver bellies, and their huge mouths bristling with teeth, from a very unscientific point of view — more as a possible victim than as a naturalist.

Happily the voracious creatures do not see well. They passed, brushing us with their brownish fins, and we escaped from a danger certainly greater than meeting a tiger full face in the forest. Half an hour later, guided by the electric light, we reached the *Nautilus*. The outside door had been left open, and Captain Nemo closed it as soon as we had entered the first cell. He then pressed a knob. I heard the pumps working in the midst of the vessel, I felt the water sinking from around me, and in a few moments the cell was entirely empty. The inside door then opened, and we entered.

Our diving dress was taken off, not without some trouble. Worn out from want of food and sleep, I returned to my room, in great wonder at this surprising excursion at the bottom of the sea.

4000 LEAGUES UNDER THE PACIFIC

T HE NEXT MORNING, the 18th of November, I had quite recovered and I went up on the platform.

I was admiring the magnificent aspect of the ocean when a number of the sailors of the *Nautilus*, all strong and healthy men, came up on the platform to draw up the nets that had been set out the night before. They used that odd language among themselves, the origin of which I could not guess.

The nets were hauled in, and I reckoned that the haul was more than 900 pounds of fish. We would have no lack of excellent food.

These productions of the sea were immediately lowered through the panel to the steward's room, some to be eaten fresh, and others pickled.

From the 4th to the 11th of December the *Nautilus* sailed over about 2000 miles.

During the daytime of the 11th of December, I was busy reading in the salon. Ned Land and Conseil watched the luminous water through the half-open panels. The *Nautilus* was motionless, at a depth of 1000 yards — a region in which large fish were seldom seen.

Conseil interrupted me. "Will master come here for a moment?" he said, in a curious voice.

"What is it, Conseil?"

"I want master to look."

I rose, went to the panels and watched.

In a full electric light, an enormous black mass seemed suspended in the water. I studied it a few minutes, then exclaimed, "A vessel!"

"Yes," replied the Canadian, "a disabled ship that has sunk perpendicularly."

Ned Land was right. We were close to a vessel whose tattered shrouds still hung about it. The hull showed that the ship had been wrecked only a short time ago. Three stumps of masts, broken off about two feet above the bridge, indicated that the vessel had had to sacrifice its masts. But, lying on its side, the hold had filled, and the wreck was heeling over to port. This skeleton of what it had so recently been a proud ship was a sad spectacle; sadder still was the sight of the bridge, where some corpses were still bound with ropes.

What a scene! We were dumb; our hearts beat fast before this shipwreck, taken as it were from life, and photographed in its last moments. And I saw already, coming toward it with hungry eyes, enormous sharks, attracted by the human flesh.

However, the *Nautilus*, starting to move, went round the submerged vessel, and in one instant I read on the stern — *"The Florida, Sunderland."*

This terrible spectacle was the forerunner of the series of maritime catastrophes that the *Nautilus* was destined to meet with in its route. We often saw the hulls of shipwrecked vessels that were rotting in the depths, and deeper down, cannons, bullets, anchors, chains.

And as we went along, we saw more and more coral islands. These islands are slowly but continuously rising and are created by the daily work of polypi. Islands might finally join and form new continents.

One day, when I was suggesting this theory to Captain Nemo, he replied coldly:

"The earth does not want new continents, but new men."

TORRES STRAITS

Dɴ THE NIGHT of the 27th or 28th of December, the *Nautilus* left the shores of Van-koro — the island which was once the scene of a search for the lost French navigator, La Perouse.

Her course was southwesterly, and in three days she had gone over the 750 leagues that separated it from La Perouse's group and the southeast point of Papua.

Early on the 1st of January, 1863, Conseil joined me on the platform.

"Master, will you permit me to wish you a happy new year?"

"Well," I said, "I accept your good wishes, and thank you for them. Only, I will ask you what you mean by a 'happy new year,' under our circumstances? Do you mean the year that will bring us to the end of our imprisonment, or the year that sees us continue this strange voyage?"

"Really, I do not know how to answer, master. We are sure to see curious things, and for the last two months we have not had time for boredom. The last marvel is always the most astonishing and if we continue I do not know how it will end. It is my opinion that we shall never again see the like. I think, then, with no offense to master, that a happy year would be one in which we could see everything."

On January 2, we had made 11,340 miles, or 5250 French leagues, since our starting point in the Japan seas. Before the ship's head stretched the dangerous shores of the Coral Sea, on the northeast coast of Australia. Our boat lay along some miles from the redoubtable bank on which Cook's vessel was lost, June 10, 1770.

I had wished to visit the reef, 360 leagues long, against which the sea, always rough, broke with great violence, with a noise like thunder. But just then the *Nautilus* plunged to a great depth, and I could see nothing of the high coral walls. I had to content myself with the different specimens of fish brought up by the nets. I saw, among others, a species of mackerel as large as a tunny, with bluish sides, and striped with transverse bands.

These fish followed us in shoals, and furnished us with very delicate food. We took also a large number of giltheads, about one and a half inches long, and flying fire fish like submarine swallows, which, in dark nights, brighten air and water with their phosphorescent light.

Two days after crossing the Coral Sea, January 4, we sighted the Papuan coasts. On this occasion, Captain Nemo informed me that his intention was to reach the Indian Ocean by the Straits of Torres.

The Torres Straits are nearly 34 leagues wide. But they are obstructed by an innumerable quantity of islands, islets, breakers, and rocks, that make its navigation almost impossible. Captain Nemo took all needful precautions to cross them. The *Nautilus* cruised at a moderate speed.

Profiting by this, I and my two companions went up on to the deserted platform. Before us was the steersman's cage, and I expected that Captain Nemo was there directing the course of the *Nautilus*. I had before me excellent charts of the Straits of Torres. Around the *Nautilus* the sea dashed furiously. The course of the

110

waves, from southeast to northwest at the rate of two and a half miles, broke on the coral that showed itself here and there.

"This is a bad sea!" remarked Ned Land.

"Indeed! and one that does not suit a boat like the *Nautilus*," I replied. "The captain must be very sure of his route, for I see there a jagged reef that might keep us here if we were to strike it."

Indeed the situation was dangerous, but the *Nautilus* seemed to slide like magic off these rocks. Veering northwest, it passed by many little known islands and atolls. Then, swerving again, it headed straight for the island of Gilboa.

It was then three in the afternoon. The *Nautilus* approached the island with its remarkable border of screw pines, and stood off at about two miles distant. Suddenly a shock overthrew me. The *Nautilus* had just touched a rock, and lay immovable, slightly to port side.

When I rose, I saw Captain Nemo and his lieutenant on the platform. They were examining the situation of the vessel, and exchanging words in their strange dialect.

Two miles, on the starboard side, appeared Gilboa, stretching from north to west like an immense arm. Toward the south and east some coral showed itself, left by the ebb of the tide. We had run aground. However, the vessel had not suffered, for her keel was solidly joined. But if she could neither glide off nor move, she ran the risk of being forever fastened to these rocks, and then Captain Nemo's submarine vessel would be done for.

I was reflecting thus, when the captain, cool and calm, always master of himself, approached me.

"An accident?" I asked.

"No — an incident."

"But an incident that will oblige you perhaps to become an inhabitant of this land which you flee?"

Captain Nemo looked at me curiously, and made a negative gesture, as much as to say that nothing would force him to set foot on *terra firma* again. Then he said:

"The *Nautilus* is not lost. It will carry you yet into the midst of the marvels of the ocean. Our voyage is only begun, and I do not wish to be deprived so soon of the honor of your company."

"However, Captain Nemo," I replied, without noticing the ironical turn of his phrase, "the *Nautilus* ran aground in open sea. Now the tides are not strong in the Pacific. If you cannot lighten the *Nautilus*, I do not see how it will be reinflated."

"The tides are not strong in the Pacific — you are right there, Professor. But in Torres Straits, one finds still a difference of a yard and a half between the level of high and low seas. Today is January 4, and in five days the moon will be full. Now, I shall be very much astonished if the moon does not increase the tide sufficiently, and render me a valuable service."

Having said this, Captain Nemo, followed by his lieutenant, descended to the interior of the *Nautilus*.

"Well, sir?" said Ned Land, who came up to me after the departure of the captain.

"Well, friend Ned, we will wait patiently for the tide on the 9th; for it appears that the moon will have the goodness to put it off again."

"Really?"

"Really."

"And this captain is not going to cast anchor at all since the tide will suffice?" said Conseil, simply.

The Canadian looked at Conseil, then shrugged his shoulders. "Sir, you may believe me when I tell you that this piece of iron will navigate neither on nor under the sea again. It is only fit to be sold for its weight. I think, therefore, that the time has come to part company with Captain Nemo."

"Friend Ned, I do not despair of this stout *Nautilus*, as you do. And in four days we shall know. Anyway, though flight might be possible if we were in sight of the English or French coasts, on the Papuan shores, it is another thing."

"But," Ned Land said, "at least there *is* an island. On that island there are trees. Under those trees are land animals, bearers of cutlets and roast beef, to which I would willingly give a trial."

"In this, friend Ned is right," said Conseil, "and I agree with him. Could not master obtain permission from his friend Captain Nemo to put us on land, if only so as not to lose the habit of treading on the solid parts of our planet?"

"I can ask him, but he will refuse."

"Will master risk it?" asked Conseil. "We shall know how to rely upon the captain's amiability."

To my great surprise Captain Nemo gave me the permission I asked for, and without even exacting from me a promise to return to the vessel. But flight across New Guinea would be very perilous, and I would not counsel Ned Land to attempt it. Better to be a prisoner on board the *Nautilus* than to fall into the hands of the natives.

At eight o'clock, armed with guns and hatchets, we left the *Nautilus*. The sea was calm, although a slight breeze blew from the land. Conseil and I rowing, we sped along quickly, and Ned steered in the straight passage that the breakers left between them. The boat was well handled, and moving rapidly.

Ned Land could not restrain his joy. He was like a prisoner who had escaped from prison.

"Meat! We are going to eat some meat — and what meat!" he cried. "Real game! I do not say that fish is not good, but a piece of fresh venison, grilled on live coals, will agreeably vary our ordinary course."

"It remains to be seen," I said, "if these forests are full of game, and if the game is not such as will hunt the hunter himself."

"Well said," replied the Canadian, whose teeth seemed sharpened like the edge of a hatchet. "But I will eat tiger — loin of tiger — if there is no other quadruped on this island. "Whatever it may be — every animal with four paws without feathers, or with two paws without feathers — will be saluted by my first shot."

"Very well! Master Land's imprudences are beginning."

"Never fear, Professor," replied the Canadian, "I do not need twenty-five minutes to obtain for you a dish of my sort."

At half-past eight the boat ran softly aground, on the sandy shore, having happily avoided the coral reef that surrounds the island of Gilboa.

A FEW DAYS ON LAND

I WAS MUCH MOVED to be treading land again. Ned Land walked heavily on the soil, as if to take possession of it. It was two months ago that we had become, according to Captain Nemo, "passengers on board the *Nautilus*," but in reality, prisoners of its commander.

In a few minutes we were within musket-shot of the coast. The interior was hidden behind a beautiful curtain of forests. Enormous trees, the trunks of which attained a height of 200 feet, were bound to each other by vines and rocked together in a light breeze. Mimosas, hibiscus and palm trees, mingled together, and under their shelter grew orchids and ferns.

But without noticing all these beautiful specimens of Papuan flora, the Canadian abandoned the agreeable for the useful. He discovered a cocoanut palm, shook down some of the fruit and broke open the cocoanuts. We drank the milk and ate the delicious white meat with a satisfaction that protested against the marine food of the *Nautilus*.

"Excellent!" said Ned Land.

"Exquisite!" replied Conseil.

"And I do not think," said the Canadian, "that he would object to our introducing a cargo of cocoanuts on board."

"I do not think he would, but he would not taste them."

"So much the worse for him," said Conseil.

"And so much the better for us," replied Ned Land. "There will be more for us."

"One word only, Master Land," I said to the harpooner, who was beginning to ravage another cocoanut tree. "Cocoanuts are good things, but before filling the canoe with them it would be wise to see if the island does not produce some fresh vegetables. They would be welcome on board the *Nautilus*."

"Master is right," replied Conseil. "And I propose to reserve three places in our vessel — one for fruits, another for vegetables, and the third for venison, of which I have not yet seen the smallest specimen."

"Conseil, we must not despair," said the Canadian.

"Let us continue," I said. "Although the island seems uninhabited, it might still contain some individuals that would be less particular than we on the nature of game."

"Ho! ho!" said Ned Land, moving his jaws. "I begin to understand the charms of cannibalism!"

"Ned! Ned! what are you saying? You, a man-eater? I shall not feel safe with you, especially as I share your cabin. I might perhaps wake one day to find myself half-devoured."

"Friend Conseil, I like you much, but not enough to eat you."

"I do not trust you," replied Conseil. "But enough. We must absolutely bring down some game to satisfy our cannibal, or else one of these fine mornings, master will find only pieces of his servant to serve him."

While we were talking, we were penetrating the somber arches of the forest, and for two hours we explored it in all directions.

Chance rewarded our search for vegetables, and one of the most useful products of the tropical zones furnished us with precious food that we missed on board. I speak of the breadfruit tree, very abundant in the island of Gilboa — and a seedless variety, which bears in Malaya the name of "rima."

Ned Land knew these fruits well. He had already eaten many during his numerous voyages, and he knew how to prepare them.

"Master," he said, "I shall die if I do not taste a little breadfruit pie."

"Taste it, friend Ned — taste it all you want. We are here to make experiments — make them."

"It won't take long," said the Canadian.

And provided with a flint, he lighted a fire of deadwood, that crackled joyously.

Conseil brought a dozen breadfruits to Ned Land, who placed them on a coal fire, after having cut them in thick slices.

"You will see how good this bread is," Ned repeated. "More so when one has been deprived of it so long. It is not even bread," added he, "but a delicate pastry. You have eaten one, Professor?"

"No, Ned."

"Well, if you do not come back for more, I am no longer the king of harpooners."

After some minutes, the fruit slices were delicately roasted. The interior looked like a white pastry, the flavor of which was like that of an artichoke. It was excellent.

"What time is it now?" asked the Canadian.

"Two o'clock at least," replied Conseil.

"How time flies on firm ground!" sighed Ned Land.

"Let us be off," replied Conseil.

We returned through the forest, and completed our collection by a raid upon the cabbage palms, that we gathered from the tops of small trees, some little beans that I recognized as the "abrou" of the Malays, and yams of a superior quality.

We were loaded down when we reached the boat.

At last, at five o'clock in the evening, loaded with our riches, we quitted the shore, and half an hour later we hailed the *Nautilus*. No one appeared; the enormous iron-plated cylinder seemed deserted. So we unloaded our provisions ourselves, I descended to my chamber, and after supper slept soundly.

The next day, January 6, there was still no sound on board, nor any sign of life. We found the small boat bobbing beside the *Nautilus*, where we had left it the day before.

We had resolved to return to the island. Ned

Land hoped to be more fortunate in hunting, and wished to visit another part of the forest.

At dawn we set off. The boat, carried by the waves, reached the island in a few minutes.

We landed, and thinking that it was better to give the Canadian the lead, we followed Ned Land, whose long limbs threatened to outdistance us. He wound along the coast toward the west. Then, fording a torrent, he reached the high plain that was bordered with great forests. We saw some kingfishers along the watercourses, but they would not let us get near them. This proved to me that these birds knew what to expect from men, and I concluded that, if the island was not inhabited, at least human beings occasionally frequented it.

After crossing a rather large prairie, we arrived at the skirts of a little wood that was enlivened by the songs and flight of a large number of birds.

"There are only birds," said Conseil.

"But they are eatable," replied the harpooner.

"I do not agree with you, friend Ned, for I see only parrots there."

"Friend Conseil," said Ned, gravely, "the parrot is like pheasant to those who have nothing else."

"And," I added, "this bird, suitably prepared, is worth knife and fork."

Indeed, under the thick foliage of this wood, a world of parrots were flying from branch to branch — parrots of all colors, and grave cockatoos. Brilliant red birds passed like scarlet flags floating on the breeze, and there were birds with the finest azure colors. In all, a variety of winged things most charming to behold.

By eleven o'clock that morning, we had climbed the mountain in the central part of the island, and had found no game to kill. Hunger drove us on.

Then Conseil, to his great surprise, made a lucky shot and secured our breakfast. He brought down a white pigeon and a wood pigeon, which he plucked and suspended from a skewer, and roasted over a fire.

While these dainty birds were cooking, Ned prepared the breadfruit. Then the wood pigeons were devoured to the bones, and declared excellent. The nutmeg, which they eat, flavors their flesh and renders it delicious eating.

"Now, Ned, what now?"

"Some four-footed game, Professor. These pigeons were only side dishes, trifles. And until I have cutlets to eat, I shall not be content."

"Let us continue hunting," said Conseil. "Let us head toward the sea. We have explored this mountain, and I think we had better return to the forest area."

That was sensible advice. After walking for one hour, we came to a forest of sago palms. Some nonpoisonous snakes glided away from us. Birds of paradise fled at our approach.

Around two o'clock in the afternoon Ned Land brought down a magnificent hog which the natives call "bari-outang."

Ned was very proud of his shot. The hog, hit by the electric ball, fell stone dead. The Canadian skinned and cleaned it properly, and cut off half a dozen cutlets to furnish us with a grilled repast in the evening. Then the hunt was resumed.

Indeed, the two friends, beating the bushes, roused a herd of kangaroo-like creatures that bounded away. But not so rapidly but what the electric guns stopped their course.

"Ah, Professor!" cried Ned Land, who was carried away by the delights of the chase, "what excellent game! What a supply for the *Nautilus*! Two! Three! Five down!"

These animals were small. They were a species of those "kangaroo rabbits" that live habitually in the hollows of trees, and whose speed is extreme. They are moderately plump, and furnish estimable food. We were very satisfied with the results of the hunt.

At six o'clock in the evening when we returned to the shore, our boat was moored to the usual place. The *Nautilus*, like a long black rock, floated in the waves two miles from the beach. Ned Land immediately went about the important business of dinner. He understood cooking and did it well. The bari-outang, grilled on the coals, soon scented the air with a delicious odor.

Indeed, the dinner was excellent. Two wood pigeons completed this extraordinary menu. The sago pastry, the breadfruit, some mangoes, and half dozen pineapples overjoyed us. My worthy companion's idea of "plain normal food" had turned into something quite exotic!

"Suppose we do not return to the *Nautilus* this evening?" said Conseil.

"Suppose we never return?" added Ned Land.

Just then a stone fell at our feet, and cut short any answer.

CAPTAIN NEMO'S THUNDERBOLT

EVEN AS WE LOOKED toward the edge of the forest, a second stone, carefully aimed, knocked the food from Conseil's hand.

"To the boat!" I cried.

There was no time to lose. About twenty natives, armed with bows and slings, appeared at the edge of the forest, hardly a hundred steps from us.

Our boat was moored about sixty feet away. The savages approached rapidly, and making hostile demonstrations. Stones and arrows fell about us.

Ned Land did not wish to leave his provisions, in spite of the danger. After seizing the pig in one hand, and two kangaroo rabbits in the other, he ran!

In two minutes we were at the boat. To load our provisions and arms, push it out to sea, and ship the oars, was the work of an instant. We had not gone two cable lengths, when a hundred savages, howling and gesticulating, entered the water up to their waists. I watched to see if this would attract some men from the *Nautilus* onto the platform. But no. The enormous machine, lying off, seemed still deserted.

Twenty minutes later we were on board. The panels were open. After making the boat fast, we entered the *Nautilus*.

"Captain!" I cried.

"Ah!" he said, "it is you, Professor? Well, have you had a good hunt?"

"Yes, Captain — but we have unfortunately brought back a troop of savages."

"Savages!" he echoed, ironically. "So you are astonished, Professor, at having set foot on a strange land and finding savages? Savages! where are there not any? Besides, are they worse than other men, these whom you call savages?"

"But, Captain — "

"How many have you counted?"

"A hundred at least."

"Professor," replied Captain Nemo, "even when *all* the natives of Papua are assembled

127

on this shore, the *Nautilus* will have nothing to fear from their attacks."

The night slipped away without event, the islanders were frightened no doubt at the sight of a monster aground in the bay. For the panels were open and would have offered an easy access to the interior of the *Nautilus*.

At six o'clock in the morning of the 8th of January, I went up onto the platform. The dawn was breaking. The island soon showed itself through the clearing fog — first the shore, than the summits.

The natives were there, more numerous than on the day before — 500 or 600 perhaps — some of them, profiting by the low water, had come onto the coral reef, at less than two cable lengths from the *Nautilus*. I could see that they were true Papuans, with athletic figures, high foreheads, white teeth, reddish tinged hair and dark, shining bodies. From the lobes of their ears, cut and distended, hung chaplets of bones. Most were naked, but the women among them wore grassy skirts. Some men wore collars of beads, red and white. Nearly all were armed with bows, arrows, slings and shields. They carried on their shoulders a sort of net containing those round stones which they cast from their slings with great skill.

One of these chiefs, nearer than the others, examined the *Nautilus*. He was, perhaps, a chief of high rank, for he wore a garment woven of banana leaves, and ornaments of brilliant colors.

They roamed about near the *Nautilus* but were not troublesome. I heard them frequently repeat the word "assai," and by their gestures I understood that they invited me to go on land, an invitation I declined.

They returned to the shore about eleven o'clock in the morning, as soon as the coral tops began to disappear under the rising tide. But I saw their numbers had increased considerably on the shore. Probably they came from the neighboring islands, or very likely from Papua. However, I had not seen a single native canoe.

Having nothing better to do, I thought of dragging a net in these beautiful limpid waters, under which I saw a profusion of shells, zoophytes, and marine plants. Moreover, it was the last day that the *Nautilus* would be in these parts, if it were to float in open sea the next day, according to Captain Nemo's promise.

I called Conseil, who brought me a little light drag, very like those for the oyster fishery. Now to work! For two hours we fished without bringing up any rarities.

But just when I expected it least, I put my hand on a wonder, very rarely met with — a left-spiral shell. Shells are all right-spiraled, with rare exceptions, and amateurs are ready to pay their weight in gold for left-spirals.

Conseil and I were absorbed in this treasure, and I was promising myself to enrich the museum with it, when a stone, struck and broke the precious object in Conseil's hand. I uttered a cry of despair!

Conseil took up his gun, and aimed at a savage who was holding his sling only ten yards away from him. I was too late to stop Conseil, and the shot broke the bracelet which encircled the arm of the savage.

"Conseil!" cried I; "Conseil!"

"Well, sir! do you not see that the cannibal began the attack?"

"A shell is not worth the life of a man," said I to him.

"Ah! the scoundrel!" cried Conseil; "I would rather he had broken my shoulder than that shell!"

Now a score of canoes surrounded the *Nautilus*. These canoes, scooped out of tree trunks were long, narrow, well adapted for speed, and were managed skillfully. I watched their advance uneasily. It was evident that these Papuans had already had dealings with the

Europeans, and knew their ships. Of this long iron cylinder anchored in the bay, without masts or chimney, they did not know what to think. Nothing good, for at first they had kept at a respectful distance. However, seeing it motionless, they now took courage, and as the canoes approached the *Nautilus*, a shower of arrows alighted on her.

I hurried down to the salon, but found no one there. I then knocked at the door that opened into the captain's room.

"Come in," he called.

"Captain," I said "the Papuans are surrounding us in their canoes, and in a few minutes we shall certainly be attacked by many hundreds of savages."

"Ah!" said Captain Nemo, quietly, "they have come with their canoes?"

"Yes, sir."

"Well, sir, we must close the hatches," he replied, calmly. "Nothing can be more simple." And pressing an electric button, he transmitted an order to the ship's crew.

"It is all done, sir," said he, after some moments. "The small boat is ready, and the hatches are closed. You do not fear, I imagine, that these gentlemen could stave in walls on which the balls of your frigate have had no effect?"

"No, Captain. But danger still exists."

"What is that, sir?"

"It is that tomorrow, at about this hour, we must open the hatches to renew the air of the *Nautilus*. Now if, at this moment, the Papuans should occupy the platform, I do not see how you could prevent them from entering."

"Then, sir, you suppose that they will board us?"

"I am certain of it."

"Well, sir, let them come. I see no reason for hindering them. I am unwilling that my visit to this island should cost the life of a single Papuan."

I turned to leave, but Captain Nemo stopped me and asked me to sit down. He questioned me with interest about our excursions on shore, and our hunting, and seemed not to understand Ned Land's craving for meat. The conversation turned to other subjects.

Then the captain arose. "Tomorrow," he said, "tomorrow, at twenty minutes to three P.M., the *Nautilus* shall float, and leave the Straits of Torres uninjured."

Having curtly pronounced these words, Captain Nemo bowed slightly, and I went back to my room. There I found Conseil, who wished to know the result of my interview with the captain.

"My boy," said I, "when I told him that the *Nautilus* was threatened by the natives of Papua, the captain answered me very sarcastically. I have but one thing to say to you — have confidence in him, and go to sleep in peace."

"Have you no need of my services, sir?"

"No, my friend. What is Ned Land doing?"

"Friend Ned is busy making a kangaroo pie which will be a marvel," answered Conseil.

At six in the morning when I rose, the hatches had not been opened. The inner air was not renewed, but the air tanks, filled and ready for any emergency, were now used, and oxygen freshened the stale atmosphere of the *Nautilus*.

I worked in my room till noon, without having seen Captain Nemo, even for an instant. On board no preparations for departure were visible.

I waited some time longer, then went into the large salon. The clock marked half-past two. In ten minutes it would be high tide and, if Captain Nemo had not made a rash promise, the *Nautilus* would be floating free. If not, many months would pass ere she could leave her bed of coral, and the now-hostile natives.

Soon, however, vibrations began to be felt

in the vessel. I heard the keel grating against the rough bottom of the coral reef.

At five-and-twenty minutes to three, Captain Nemo appeared in the salon.

"We are ready to leave," said he.

"Ah!" replied I.

"I have given the order to open the hatches."

"And the Papuans?"

"The Papuans?" answered Captain Nemo, slightly shrugging his shoulders.

"Will they not come inside the *Nautilus*?"

"How?"

"By leaping through the hatches you have opened," I said.

"Professor," quietly answered Captain Nemo, "They will not enter the *Nautilus*, even if the hatches are open. Come and you will see."

At the central staircase Ned Land and Conseil were watching some of the ship's crew, who were opening the hatches. Frightening cries of rage sounded outside.

The port lids were pulled down. Twenty savage faces appeared. But the first Papuan who placed his hand on the stair rail seemed struck from behind by some invisible force. He uttered a fearful cry and plunged into the water.

Ten of his companions met with the same fate, and followed him overboard.

Ned Land, carried away by his violent instincts, rushed on to the staircase. But the moment he seized the rail with both hands, he was thrown back down.

"I've been struck by a thunderbolt!" he cried, with an oath.

This explained all. The stair rail was a metal cable, charged with electricity from the deck and communicating with the platform. Whoever touched it felt a powerful shock.

At this moment, the *Nautilus,* raised by the last waves of the tide, quitted her coral bed exactly at the fortieth minute fixed by the captain. Her propellers beat the waters as her speed increased gradually. So sailing on the surface of the ocean, safe and sound, she left the dangerous passes of the Strait of Torres.

"AEGRI SOMNIA"

ON THE 13TH OF JANUARY, Captain Nemo
reached the Sea of Timor, and took his bearings by the island of that name in 122° long.

From this point, the *Nautilus*'s direction was
southwest, toward the Indian Ocean. Where
would Captain Nemo's fancy carry us next?
Along the coast of Asia? Or would he swing
toward the shores of Europe?

On the 16th January, the *Nautilus* was floating a few yards beneath the surface of the
waves. Her electric apparatus remained inac-
tive, and she drifted at the whim of the currents. I supposed that the crew was making
engine repairs.

My companions and I then witnessed a curious spectacle. The hatches of the salon were

open. But the beacon light of the *Nautilus* was not in action and the waters were dim. The largest fish appeared to me no more than a scarcely defined shadow. So when the *Nautilus* was suddenly surrounded by light, I thought at first that the beacon had been turned on, and was casting its electric radiance into the ocean's waters. I was mistaken, and soon saw my error.

The *Nautilus* was now floating in the midst of a phosphorescent bed, which, in this dimness, became quite dazzling. It was produced by myriads of luminous animalculae, whose brilliancy were increased as they glided over the metallic hull of the vessel. I was surprised to see lightning in the midst of these luminous sheets!

For several hours the *Nautilus* floated in these brilliant waves, and our admiration increased as we watched. This dazzling spectacle was enchanting! Perhaps some atmospheric condition increased the intensity of this phenomenon — a storm that churned up the surface of the ocean. But, at this depth, the *Nautilus* was untouched by its fury, and reposed peacefully in a dazzling side effect of the gale.

So we progressed, charmed each day by some

new marvel. Days passed rapidly. Ned, according to habit, tried to vary the diet on board. Like snails, we were fixed in our shell, and I declare it is easy to lead a snail's life.

We were beginning to think no longer of the life we had led on land. Then something happened to recall us to the strangeness of our situation.

On the 18th of January, the *Nautilus* was in 105° long. and 15° S. lat. The weather was threatening, the sea rough and rolling. There was a strong east wind.

I went up onto the platform just as the second lieutenant was taking the measure of the sun's angle, and I waited, according to habit, till the daily phrase was said. But on this day it was exchanged for another phrase no more easily understood. Almost directly, I saw Captain Nemo appear with a spyglass, looking toward the horizon.

For some minutes he was immovable, never taking his eye from his point of observation. Then he lowered the spyglass and exchanged a few words with his lieutenant. The latter seemed to react with strong emotion. Captain Nemo, always in command of himself, appeared cool.

For myself I had looked carefully in the direction indicated without seeing anything. Sky and water extended to the clear line of the horizon.

However, Captain Nemo walked from one end of the platform to the other without looking at me, perhaps without seeing me. His step was firm but less regular than usual. He stopped sometimes, crossed his arms, and observed the sea. What could he be looking for on that immense expanse? The *Nautilus* was then some hundreds of miles from the nearest coast.

Meanwhile, the lieutenant had taken up the spyglass, and examined the horizon earnestly, going and coming, stamping his foot and showing more nervous agitation than his superior officer.

Upon an order from Captain Nemo, the engine increased its propelling power.

Just then, the lieutenant drew the captain's attention again. The latter stopped walking and directed his spyglass toward the spot indicated. He looked long. I felt very much puzzled, and went down to the drawing room to take out an excellent telescope that I generally used. Then, from the edge of the watchlight that jutted out from the front of the platform, I set myself to look over all the line of the sky and sea.

But no sooner had I raised the instrument than it was quickly snatched out of my hands.

I turned round. Captain Nemo was before me but I did not know him. His face was changed. His eyes flashed sullenly. His teeth were set, his body stiff, fists clenched, and head shrunk between his shoulders. My telescope, fallen from his hands, had rolled at his feet.

Did this strange person imagine that I had discovered some forbidden secret? No! *I* was not the object of his hatred, for he was not looking at me. His eye was steadily fixed upon some far point of the horizon.

At last Captain Nemo recovered himself. His agitation subsided. He addressed some words in a foreign language to his lieutenant, then turned to me. "Professor," he said, "I require you to keep one of the conditions that bind you to me."

"What is it, Captain?"

"You must be confined with your companions, until I think fit to release you."

"You are the master," I replied, looking steadily at him. "But may I ask you one question?"

"None, sir."

There was nothing to say to this. I went down to the cabin occupied by Ned Land and Conseil, and told them the captain's words.

There was no time for argument. Four of the crew waited at the door, and conducted us to that cell where we had passed our first night on board the *Nautilus*.

Ned Land would have objected, but the door was shut upon him. Then he exclaimed, "Hallo! Breakfast is ready."

And indeed the table was laid. Evidently Captain Nemo had given this order at the same time that he had hastened the speed of the *Nautilus*.

"Will master permit me to suggest that master breakfasts. It is wise, for we do not know what may happen."

"You are right, Conseil."

"Unfortunately," said Ned Land, "they have only given us the usual ship's fare."

"Friend Ned," asked Conseil, "what would you have said if the breakfast had been entirely forgotten?"

We sat down to table. The meal was eaten in silence.

Just then, the globe that lighted the cell went out and left us in total darkness. Ned Land and Conseil went off into a heavy sleep. And in spite of my efforts to keep my eyes open, they *would* close. A painful suspicion seized me — something had been mixed with the food we had just taken! Imprisonment was not enough to conceal Captain Nemo's projects from us. Sleep was necessary!

I then heard the panels shut. The movement of the sea, which caused a slight rolling motion, ceased. Had the *Nautilus* left the surface of the ocean? Had it gone back to the motionless bed of water? I tried to resist sleep. It was impossible. My breathing grew weak. I felt cold freeze my stiffened and half-paralyzed limbs. My eyelids, like leaden caps, fell over my eyes. I could not raise them — I slept.

THE CORAL KINGDOM

THE NEXT DAY I woke with my head clear. To
my great surprise I was in my own room. My
companions, no doubt, were back in their cabin.

Was I free again or a prisoner? Quite free.
I opened the door, went to the half-deck, went
up the central stairs. The panels, shut the evening before, were open. I went onto the platform.

Ned Land and Conseil waited there for me.
I questioned them. They knew nothing. Lost in
a heavy sleep in which they had been totally
unconscious, they had been astonished at finding themselves in their cabin.

As for the *Nautilus*, it seemed quiet and
mysterious as ever. It floated on the surface of

the waves at a moderate pace. Nothing seemed changed on board.

The second lieutenant then came onto the platform and gave the usual order below.

As for Captain Nemo, he did not appear.

Of the people on board, I only saw the steward, who served me with his usual silent regularity.

About two o'clock, I was in the drawing room, busied in arranging my notes, when the captain opened the door and appeared. I bowed. He nodded in return, without speaking. I resumed my work, hoping that he would perhaps give me some explanation of the events of the preceding night. He made none. I looked at him. He seemed tired. His heavy eyes had not been refreshed by sleep. His face looked very sorrowful. He walked to and fro, sat down and got up again, took up a chance book, put it down, consulted his instruments without taking his habitual notes, and seemed restless and uneasy. At last, he came up to me, and said:

"Are you a doctor, Professor?"

I so little expected such a question, that I stared some time at him without answering.

"Are you a doctor?" he repeated. "Several of your colleagues have studied medicine."

"Well," said I, "I am a doctor and surgeon. I practiced several years."

"Very well, sir."

My answer had evidently satisfied the captain. But not knowing what he would say next, I waited for other questions.

"Professor, will you consent to prescribe for one of my men?" he asked.

"Is he ill?"

"Yes."

"I am ready to follow you."

"Come, then."

My heart beat hard. I do not know why. I saw a certain connection between the illness of one of the crew and the events of the day before. This mystery interested me at least as much as the sick man.

Captain Nemo conducted me to a cabin near the sailors' quarters. There, on a bed, lay a man about forty years of age.

I leaned over him. He was not only ill, he was wounded. His head, swathed in bandages covered with blood, lay on a pillow. I undid the bandages, and the wounded man looked at me with his large eyes and gave no sign of pain. It was a horrible wound. The skull, shattered by some deadly weapon, left the brain exposed, which was much injured. Clots of blood had formed in the bruised and broken mass, in color like the dregs of wine.

His breathing was slow, and some spasmodic

movements of the muscles agitated his face. I felt his pulse. It was unsteady. I readjusted the bandages on his head, and turned to Captain Nemo.

"What caused this wound?" I asked.

"What does it matter?" he replied, evasively. "A shock has broken one of the engine levers. It struck myself too. But your opinion as to his state?"

I hesitated before giving it.

"You may speak," said the captain. "This man does not understand French."

I gave a last look at the wounded man.

"He will be dead in two hours."

"Can nothing save him?"

"Nothing."

Captain Nemo's hand contracted, and some tears glistened in his eyes, which I had thought incapable of shedding any.

"You can go now, Professor," said the captain.

I left him in the dying man's cabin, and returned to my room much affected by this scene. During the whole day, I was haunted by uncomfortable suspicions, and that night I slept badly. Between my broken dreams, I fancied I heard distant sounds like the notes of a funeral psalm.

The next morning I went on the bridge.

Captain Nemo was there before me. As soon as he saw me he came to me.

"Professor, will it be convenient to you to make a submarine excursion today?"

"With my companions?" I asked.

"If they like."

"We obey your orders, Captain."

"Will you be so good then as to make ready?"

By half-past eight in the morning we were equipped for this new excursion, and provided with the two contrivances for light and breathing. The double door was open, and accompanied by Captain Nemo, who was followed by a dozen of the crew, we set foot, at a depth of about 30 feet, on the solid bottom on which the *Nautilus* rested.

A slight declivity ended in an uneven bottom, at 15 fathoms depth. This bottom differed entirely from the one I had visited on my first excursion under the waters of the Pacific Ocean. Here, there was no fine sand, no submarine prairies, no sea-forest. It was the coral kingdom.

The light showed a thousand charming coral varieties. It played in the midst of the brightly colored branches. I was tempted to gather their fresh blossoms, ornamented with delicate tentacles, some full-blown, others just budding.

Small fish, swimming swiftly, touched them lightly, like flights of birds. But if my hand approached these living flowers, these animated sensitive plants, the whole colony took alarm. The white petals re-entered their red cases, the flowers faded as I looked, and the bush changed into a block of stony knobs.

Chance had placed me beside the most precious specimens of this zoophyte. This coral was more valuable than that found in the Mediterranean, on the coasts of France, Italy, and Barbary. Its tints justified the poetical names of "Flower of Blood," and "Froth of Blood," that trade has given to its most beautiful productions. The coral in this place would make the fortunes of a company of coral divers.

The light from our lamps produced sometimes magical effects, following the rough outlines of the natural arches, and pendants, like lusters, were tipped with points of fire.

At last, after walking two hours, we had attained a depth of about 300 yards, that is to say, the extreme depth at which coral begins to form. But there was no isolated bush, nor modest brushwood, at the bottom of these lofty trees. It was an immense forest of large mineral vegetations, enormous petrified trees adorned with clouds and reflections. We passed freely under their high branches, lost in the shade of the waves.

Captain Nemo had stopped. I and my companions halted, and turning round, I saw his men were forming a semicircle round their chief. Watching attentively, I observed that four of them carried on their shoulders an object of an oblong shape.

We occupied, in this place, the center of a vast glade surrounded by the lofty foliage of the submarine forest. Our lamps threw a sort of clear twilight that lengthened the shadows on the sea bottom. At the end of the glade the darkness increased, and was only lightened by little sparks reflected by the points of coral.

Ned Land and Conseil were near me. We watched a strange scene.

In the midst of the glade, on a pedestal of rocks roughly piled up, stood a cross of coral, that one might have thought were made of petrified blood.

Upon a sign from Captain Nemo, one of the men advanced. At some feet from the cross, he began to dig a hole with a pickaxe that he took from his belt. I understood all! This glade was a cemetery, this hole a tomb, this oblong object the body of the man who had died in the night! The captain and his men had come to bury their companion in this general resting place, at the bottom of this inaccessible ocean!

The grave was being dug slowly. The fish fled on all sides while their retreat was being disturbed. I heard the strokes of the pickaxe, which sparkled when it hit upon some flint lost at the bottom of the waters. The hole was soon large and deep enough to receive the body. Then the bearers approached. The body, wrapped in white, was lowered into the grave. Captain Nemo, with his arms crossed on his breast, and all the others, knelt in prayer.

The grave was then filled in and formed a slight mound. When this was done, Captain Nemo and his men rose. Then, approaching the grave, they knelt again, and all extended their hands in a sign of a last good-bye. Then the funeral procession returned to the *Nautilus*, passing under the arches of the forest, in the midst of thickets of coral. At last the lights on board appeared, and their luminous track guided us to the *Nautilus*. At one o'clock we had returned.

As soon as I had changed my clothes, I went up onto the platform. Captain Nemo joined me. I rose and said, "So, as I said he would, this man died in the night?"

"Yes, Professor."

"And he rests now, near his companions, in the coral cemetery?"

"Yes, forgotten by all else, but not by us. We dug the grave, and the coral seal our dead for eternity." And burying his face quickly in his hands, he tried in vain to suppress a sob. Then he added, "Our peaceful cemetery is there, some hundred feet below the surface of the waves."

"Your dead sleep quietly, at least, Captain, out of the reach of sharks."

"Yes, sir, of sharks and *men*," gravely replied the captain.

PART II

W E NOW COME to the second part of our journey under the sea. The first ended with the
moving scene in the coral cemetery, which left
a deep impression on my mind.

THE INDIAN OCEAN

THE EVENTS which took place before our visit to the coral cemetery had made me ponder. I remembered the captain's fury when he snatched the spyglass from me as I raised it to sweep the horizon. I thought more about our mysterious imprisonment, and the drugged breakfast that had chained us in sleep; and then about the man who was mortally wounded by an unaccountable shock to the *Nautilus*. All this set my thinking on a new track:

Was Captain Nemo really satisfied merely with avoiding men? Was his formidable submarine *only* a means of maintaining his instinct of freedom? Or was it also the instrument of some terrible revenge?

But these dark thoughts ceased to trouble me as the *Nautilus* glided on through the splendid tropical waters at between fifty and a hundred fathoms deep.

We were now furrowing the depths of the Indian Ocean, a vast sea whose waters are remarkably clear and transparent.

To anyone but myself, who had a great love for the sea, the hours would have seemed long and monotonous. But the daily walks on the platform when I steeped myself in the ocean air, the sight of the rich waters through the windows of the salon, the books in the library and the compiling of my memoirs took up all my time and left me not a moment of boredom.

On the 26th of January, we cut the equator at the eighty-second meridian, and entered the northern hemisphere.

During the day, a formidable troop of sharks accompanied us, terrible creatures that multiply in these seas, and make the waters very dangerous. There were "cestracio philippi" sharks, with brown backs and whitish bellies, armed with eleven rows of teeth — called eyed sharks because the throat is marked with a large black spot surrounded with white like an eye. There were also some Isabella sharks, with rounded snouts marked with dark spots. These powerful creatures often hurled themselves at the windows of the salon with great violence. At such times Ned Land longed to go to the surface and harpoon the monsters, particularly the huge tiger-sharks. These last seemed to excite Ned most. But the *Nautilus*, accelerating speed, easily left even the fastest monsters behind.

The 27th of January, at the entrance of the vast Bay of Bengal, we met repeatedly a forbidding spectacle — dead bodies floating on the surface of the water. They were the dead of the Indian villages, carried by the Ganges to the sea, and which the vultures, the only undertakers of the country, had not been able to devour. But the sharks did not fail to help them at their funeral work.

A NOVEL PROPOSAL OF CAPTAIN NEMO'S

ON THE 28TH OF FEBRUARY, the Nautilus surfaced at noon, in 9° 4′ N. lat. There was land in sight about eight miles to westward, and the first thing I noticed was a range of mountains about 2000 feet high, the shapes of which were most fanciful. On taking the bearings, I knew that we were nearing the Island of Ceylon, the pearl which hangs from the lobe of the Indian Peninsula.

Captain Nemo and his second appeared at this moment. The captain glanced at the map. Then, turning to me, he said, "The Island of Ceylon, noted for its pearl-fisheries. Would you like to visit one of them, Professor?"

"Certainly, Captain."

"Well, the thing is easy to arrange. I will give orders to make for the Gulf of Manaar, which we shall reach during the night."

The captain said something to his second, who immediately went out. Soon the manometer showed that the *Nautilus* was about 30 feet deep.

"Well, sir," said Captain Nemo, "you and your companions shall visit the Banks of Manaar, and if by chance some fisherman should be there, we shall see him at work."

"Agreed, Captain!"

"By the way, Professor, you are not afraid of sharks?"

"Sharks!" I exclaimed. "I admit, Captain, that I am not yet very familiar with that kind of fish."

"We are accustomed to them," replied Captain Nemo, "and in time you will be too. However, we shall be armed, and on the way we may be able to hunt some of that tribe. It is interesting. So, till tomorrow, sir, and early."

This said in a careless tone, Captain Nemo left the salon. As for myself, I passed my hand over my forehead, on which stood large drops of cold perspiration. Hunting otters in submarine forests, as we did in the island of Crespo will pass, but wandering around in the sea where one is almost certain to meet sharks, is quite another thing!

At this moment, Conseil and the Canadian entered. They knew not what awaited them!

"Faith, sir," said Ned Land, "your Captain Nemo has just made us a very pleasant offer."

"Ah!" said I, "you know?"

"If agreeable to you, sir," interrupted Conseil, "the commander of the *Nautilus* has invited us to visit the magnificent Ceylon fisheries tomorrow, in your company; he did it kindly, and behaved like a real gentleman."

"He said nothing more?"

"Nothing more, sir, except that he had already spoken to you of this little walk."

"Sir," said Conseil, "would you give us some details of the pearl-fishery?"

"As to the fishing itself," I asked, "or the incidents which surround it? Which?"

"On the fishing," replied the Canadian. "Before entering upon new ground, it is as well to know something about it."

"Very well. Sit down, my friends, and I will tell you."

Ned and Conseil seated themselves and the first thing the Canadian asked was:

"Sir, what is a pearl?"

"The particular mollusk which secretes the

pearl is the *Pearl oyster,*" I said. "The pearl is nothing but a nacreous formation, deposited in a globular form, either adhering to the oyster shell, or buried in the folds of the creature. On the shell it is fast; in the flesh it is loose. But it always has for a kernel a small hard substance — maybe a barren egg, maybe a grain of sand — around which the pearly matter deposits itself year after year in thin layers."

"Are many pearls found in the oyster?" asked Conseil.

"Yes. One oyster has been mentioned, though I allow myself to doubt it, as having contained no less than a hundred and fifty sharks."

"A hundred and fifty *sharks!*" exclaimed Ned Land.

"Did I say sharks?" said I, hurriedly. "I meant to say a hundred and fifty *pearls.*"

"Is this pearl-fishery dangerous?" Conseil asked.

"No," I answered, quickly. "Not if certain precautions are taken."

"What does one risk?" said Ned Land.

Trying to take Captain Nemo's careless tone, I said, "Are you afraid of sharks, Ned?"

"I!" replied the Canadian. "A harpooner by profession? It is my trade to make light of them."

"But," said I, "it is not a question of fishing

for them with an iron swivel, hoisting them into the vessel, cutting off their tails with a blow of a chopper, ripping them up, and throwing their hearts into the sea!"

"Then, it is a question of — "

"Precisely," said I.

"In the water?" asked Ned.

"In the water."

"Well, but with a good harpoon. . . . You know, sir, these sharks are ill-fashioned beasts. They must turn on their bellies to seize you, and in the time. . . ."

Ned Land had a way of saying "seize," which made my blood run cold.

"Well, and you, Conseil, what do you think of sharks?"

"Me!" said Conseil. "I will be frank, sir."

"So much the better," thought I.

"If you, sir, mean to face the sharks, I do not see why your faithful servant should not face them with you."

A PEARL OF TEN MILLIONS

THE NEXT MORNING at four o'clock, I was awakened by the steward, whom Captain Nemo had placed at my service. I rose hurriedly, dressed, and went into the salon.

Captain Nemo was awaiting me.

"Professor," said he, "are you ready to start?"

"I am ready."

"Then, please to follow me."

"And my companions, Captain?"

"They have been told, and are waiting."

"Are we not to put on our divers' suits?" I asked.

"Not yet. I have not allowed the *Nautilus* to

come too near this coast, and we are some distance from the Manaar Banks. But the boat is ready. It carries our diving apparatus, which we will put on when we begin our underwater journey."

Captain Nemo conducted me to the central staircase, which led on to the platform. Ned and Conseil were already there, delighted at the idea of the "pleasure party" which was preparing. Five sailors from the *Nautilus*, with their oars, waited in the boat which had been made fast against the side.

The night was still dark. Layers of clouds covered the sky, allowing but few stars to be seen. I looked on the side where the land lay, and saw nothing but a dark line enclosing three parts of the horizon, from southwest to northwest. The *Nautilus*, having returned during the night up the western coast of Ceylon, was now west of the bay, or rather gulf, formed by the mainland and the Island of Manaar. There, under the dark waters, stretched the oyster bank, an inexhaustible field of pearls, over 20 miles long.

Captain Nemo, Ned Land, Conseil, and I took our places in the stern of the boat. The master went to the tiller, his four companions leaned on their oars, and we sheered off.

The boat was headed south. The oarsmen's strokes were strong and rhythmic, in ten-second intervals, according to the method generally adopted in the navy. The liquid drops from the oars struck the dark depths of the waves crisply like spats of melted lead.

We were silent. What was Captain Nemo thinking of? Perhaps of the land he was approaching, which he found too near for comfort.

Six o'clock! It was suddenly daylight, with that rapidity peculiar to the tropical regions of sudden dawns and short twilights. Then the solar rays pierced the clouds, piled up on the eastern horizon, and the radiant orb rose rapidly. Now I saw the land distinctly.

The boat neared Manaar Island, which was rounded to the south. Captain Nemo rose from his seat and watched. At a sign from him the anchor was dropped in water a little more than a yard deep.

"Here we are, Professor," said Captain Nemo. "You see that enclosed bay? Here, in a month, will be assembled the numerous fishing boats of the exporters, and these are the waters their divers will ransack so boldly. Happily, the bay is well situated for that kind of fishing. It is sheltered from the strongest winds. The sea is never very rough here, which makes it favorable for the diver's work. We will now put on our suits, and begin our walk."

With the help of the sailors I put on my heavy sea suit. Captain Nemo and my companions were also dressing. None of the *Nautilus* men were to accompany us.

Soon we were enclosed in indiarubber clothing, with the air tanks fixed to our backs by braces. Before putting my head into the copper helmet, I asked the captain if we were to carry lamps.

"They would be useless," he replied. "We are going to no great depth, and the solar rays will be enough to light our walk. Besides, it would not be wise to carry electric light in these waters. Its brilliancy might attract some of the dangerous inhabitants of the coast."

As Captain Nemo said these words, I turned to Conseil and Ned Land. But my two friends had already encased their heads in the metal caps, and they could neither hear nor answer.

One last question remained to ask of Captain Nemo.

"And our arms?" asked I; "our guns?"

"Guns? What for? Here is a strong blade, put it in your belt, and we start."

I looked at my companions. They were armed

like us, and, more than that, Ned Land was brandishing the enormous harpoon which he had placed in the boat before leaving the *Nautilus*.

An instant later we were standing, one behind the other, in about six feet of water upon an even sand. Captain Nemo made a sign with his hand, and we followed him.

Over our feet rose shoals of fish which have no other fins but their tail. I recognized the Javanese, a real serpent two and a half feet long, of a livid color underneath, and which might easily be mistaken for a conger eel if it were not for the golden stripes on its side.

The heightening sun lit the waters more and more, and we could see the terrain change by degrees. To the fine sand succeeded a perfect causeway of boulders, covered with a carpet of mollusks and zoophytes.

At about seven o'clock we found ourselves at last surveying the oyster banks, on which the pearl oysters are produced by millions.

Captain Nemo pointed with his hand to the enormous heap of oysters, and Ned Land hastened to fill a net which he carried by his side with some of the most promising specimens. But we could not stop. We must follow the captain, who seemed to follow paths known only to himself. The ground was rising, and sometimes, on holding up my arm, I would see that it was above the surface of the sea. Then the level of the bank would sink suddenly.

At this moment there opened before us a large grotto carpeted with submarine flora. At first its vague transparency became nothing more than drowned light.

Captain Nemo entered. We followed, and my eyes were soon accustomed to the relative darkness. I could distinguish arches springing from natural pillars.

Why had our guide led us to the bottom of this submarine crypt? I was soon to know. After a sharp descent our feet trod the bottom of a kind of circular pit. There Captain Nemo stopped, and with his hand indicated an object I had not yet perceived. It was an oyster of extraordinary dimensions — a gigantic tridacne, the breadth of which was more than two yards and a half! As I drew nearer to this extraordinary mollusk, I estimated that its weight was 600 pounds, and that it would contain 30 pounds of meat.

Captain Nemo was evidently well acquainted with the existence of this bivalve. The shells were partly open and the captain put his dagger between to prevent them from closing.

Then with his hand he raised the membrane with its fringed edges, and there, between the folds, I saw a gigantic pearl! It was almost the size of a cocoanut, and its globular shape, perfect clarity and admirable luster made it altogether a jewel of incredible value. I stretched out my hand to touch it. But the captain stopped me, quickly withdrew his dagger, and the two shells closed. I understood Captain Nemo's intention. In leaving this pearl, he was allowing it to grow slowly. Each year the secretions of the mollusk would add new layers. I estimated its value even then at three million dollars.

We proceeded on our walk for a few minutes, when Captain Nemo stopped short, and motioned us to crouch beside him in a deep crevice of the rock. He pointed to one area of the waters, which I watched attentively.

About 15 feet from me a shadow appeared and sank to the ocean floor. Again I thought of sharks, but it was a man, an East Indian fisherman who, I suppose, had come to glean before the big harvest began. I could see the bottom of his canoe anchored some feet above his head. He would dive and go up repeatedly. He held a stone between his feet which was fastened by a rope to his boat, and this helped him to descend more rapidly. This and a bag were all his equipment. Reaching the bottom, about 15 feet below, he knelt down and filled his bag with oysters. Then he went up, emptied it and began the operation once more, which took about thirty seconds.

The diver did not see us hidden in the shadow of the rock. And how could this poor man ever dream that men, beings like himself, could be there under water with him, observing his movements? Several times he went up and dived again. He did not carry away more than ten oysters at each plunge, for he had to pull them from the bank to which they were fastened. And how many of those oysters, for which he risked his life, had no pearl in them! I watched him closely, his maneuvers were well coordinated; and for half an hour no danger appeared to threaten him.

Then suddenly, while he was on the bottom I saw him make a gesture of terror, rise and spring toward the ocean's surface.

How well I understood his dread! A gigantic shadow had appeared above the unfortunate diver. A shark of enormous size was cutting in, its jaws open. I was numb with horror and unable to move.

The voracious creature shot toward the Indian, who threw himself on one side to avoid the shark's fins. But its tail struck his chest and knocked him to the ocean floor. The shark returned and flipped on its back, preparing to cut the Indian in two. I saw Captain Nemo rise suddenly. Dagger in hand, he walked toward the monster, ready for direct combat. Just as the shark was about to snap the unhappy fisherman in two, it saw its new adversary, and turning over again, made straight toward him.

I can still see Captain Nemo as he waited for the shark with admirable coolness. When it rushed at him, he threw himself on one side with wonderful quickness and buried his dagger deep in its side. But the danger was not yet over. A terrible struggle followed.

The shark had seemed to roar, if I might say so. Blood poured from its wound. The sea was dyed red, and I could see nothing. Nothing, until a moment later I saw the undaunted captain hanging onto one of the creature's fins, struggling with the monster. He was dealing successive blows at his enemy, yet unable to give the decisive one.

I wanted to go to the captain's assistance, but I was rooted to the spot with horror.

Then the captain sank, overpowered by the enormous mass. The shark's jaws opened wide, and it might have been all over with the captain but for Ned Land, who suddenly rushed toward the shark and struck it with his harpoon.

The waves were stained a brilliant red as the shark churned them with indescribable fury. But Ned Land's aim was true. The monster was struck to the heart, and these were its death throes.

Ned Land had meanwhile disentangled the captain, who was not wounded. The captain went over to the Indian. He took him in his arms, and, with a strong push of his toes, mounted to the surface.

All three of us followed, feeling we had been saved by a miracle, and in a few seconds we reached the fisherman's boat.

Captain Nemo's first thought was to resusitate the unfortunate man. I did not think he could succeed. The poor man's immersion had not been long, but the blow from the shark's tail might have injured him fatally.

Happily, with the captain's and Conseil's ministrations, I saw consciousness return by degrees. The diver opened his eyes. Imagine his surprise, his terror even, at seeing four great copper heads leaning over him! And what must he have thought when Captain

Nemo, drawing from his pocket a bag of pearls, placed it in his hand! This munificent charity the poor pearl diver accepted with a trembling hand. His wondering eyes showed that he knew not to what superhuman beings he owed both fortune and life.

At a sign from the captain we returned to the water, and, in about half an hour, to the anchor which held the long boat of the *Nautilus*.

Once on board, we each, with the help of the sailors, got rid of the heavy copper helmets.

Captain Nemo's first word was to the Canadian.

"Thank you, Master Land," said he.

"It was repayment, Captain," replied Ned Land. "I owed you that."

A ghastly smile passed across the captain's face, then:

"To the *Nautilus*," said he.

The boat flew over the waves. Some minutes later, we saw the dead shark's floating body. By the black marking of the fins, I recognized the terrible melanopteron of the Indian Ocean. It was more than 25 feet long. It was an adult, as was indicated by its six rows of teeth placed in a triangle in the upper jaw.

While we were contemplating it, a dozen of these voracious beasts appeared round the boat. Without noticing us, they threw themselves upon the dead body and fought with one another for the pieces.

At half-past eight we were again on board the *Nautilus*. There I reflected on the incidents which had taken place in our excursion to the Manaar Banks.

Two conclusions I must inevitably draw from it — one, the unparalleled courage of Captain Nemo. The other, his devotion to a human being — a representative of that race from which he fled beneath the sea. Whatever he might say, this strange man had not yet succeeded in entirely crushing his heart.

When I made this observation to him, he answered in a slightly moved tone:

"That Indian, sir, is an inhabitant of an oppressed country. And I am still, and shall be, to my last breath, one of them!"

THE RED SEA

B Y THE 29TH OF JANUARY, we had made 16,-220 miles, or 7500 French leagues from our starting point in the Japanese Seas.

The next day when the *Nautilus* went to the surface of the ocean, there was no land in sight. Its course was N.N.E., in the direction of the Sea of Oman, between Arabia and the Indian Peninsula, which serves as an outlet to the Persian Gulf. Where was Captain Nemo taking us? I could not say. When the Canadian came to me asking where we were going, I said:

"We are going where our captain's fancy takes us, Master Ned."

"His fancy cannot take us far, then," said the Canadian. "The Persian Gulf has no outlet."

"Very well, then, we will come back again, Master Land. And if, after the Persian Gulf, the *Nautilus* would like to visit the Red Sea, the Straits of Bab-el-mandeb are there to give us entrance."

"I need not tell you, sir," said Ned Land, "that the Red Sea is as much closed as the Gulf, as the Isthmus of Suez is not yet cut; and if it was, a boat as mysterious as ours would not risk going through the locks of a canal. And again, the Red Sea is not the road to take us back to Europe."

"But I never said we were going back to Europe."

"What do you suppose, then?"

"I suppose that, after visiting the curious coasts of Arabia and Egypt, the *Nautilus* will go down the Indian Ocean again, and perhaps cross the Channel of Mozambique so as to gain the Cape of Good Hope."

"And once at the Cape of Good Hope?" asked the Canadian, with peculiar emphasis.

"Well, we shall penetrate into that Atlantic which we do not yet know. Ah! friend Ned, you are getting tired of this journey under the sea. For my part, I shall be sorry to see the end of a voyage which it is given to so few men to make."

For four days, till the 3d of February, the *Nautilus* scoured the Sea of Oman, at various speeds and at various depths. It seemed to move at random, as if the captain were uncertain as to which road it should follow.

The 5th of February we at last entered the Gulf of Aden, a perfect funnel through which the Indian waters entered the Red Sea.

The 6th of February, the *Nautilus* floated in sight of Aden, perched upon a promontory which a narrow isthmus joins to the mainland.

I certainly thought that Captain Nemo, at this point, would turn around. But I was mistaken.

The next day, the 7th of February, we entered the Straits of Bab-el-mandeb, the name of which, in the Arab tongue, means "The gate of tears."

Twenty miles in breadth, it is only thirty-two in length. And for the *Nautilus*, starting at full speed, the crossing was scarcely the work at an hour. But I saw nothing. There were too many English or French steamers furrowing this narrow passage, for the *Nautilus* to venture to show itself. At last, about noon, we were in the waters of the Red Sea.

I would not even seek to understand why

177

Captain Nemo decided upon entering the gulf. But I quite approved of his decision. Our speed was lessened; sometimes the *Nautilus* surfaced, sometimes it dived to avoid a vessel, and thus I was able to observe both the upper and lower parts of this curious sea.

What pleasant hours I passed at the window of the salon! What new specimens of submarine flora and fauna did I admire under the brightness of our electric lantern!

There grew sponges of all shapes. They certainly justified the names of baskets, cups, distaffs, elk's horns, lion's feet, peacock's tails, and Neptune's-gloves, which have been given to them by fishermen.

The 9th of February, the *Nautilus* floated in the broadest part of the Red Sea, between Souakin, on the west coast, and Koomfidah, on the east coast — with a diameter of 90 miles.

That day at noon, after the bearings were taken, Captain Nemo mounted the platform where I happened to be. As soon as he saw me he said, "Well, sir, does this Red Sea please you? Have you sufficiently observed the wonders it covers, its fishes, its zoophytes, its garden sponges, and its forests of coral? Did you catch a glimpse of the towns on its borders?"

"Yes, Captain Nemo," I replied, "and the

178

Nautilus is wonderfully fitted for such a study. Ah! it is an intelligent boat!"

"Yes, sir, intelligent and invulnerable," he replied. "It required many ages to find out the mechanical power of steam. Who knows if, in another hundred years, we may not see a second *Nautilus*? Progress is slow, Professor Aronnax."

"It is true," I answered. "Your boat is at least a century before its time, perhaps an era. What a misfortune that the secret of such an invention should die with its inventor!"

Captain Nemo did not reply. After some minutes' silence he continued.

"Unfortunately, I cannot take you through the Suez Canal. But you will be able to see the long jetty of Port Said after tomorrow, when we shall be in the Mediterranean."

"The Mediterranean!" I exclaimed.

"Yes, sir; does that astonish you?"

"What astonishes me is to think that we shall be there the day after tomorrow."

"Indeed?"

"Yes, Captain, although by this time I ought not to be surprised at anything, that now I have been on board your boat."

"But the cause of this surprise?"

"Well, it is the fearful speed you will have

to put on the *Nautilus,* if the day after tomorrow she is to be in the Mediterranean, having made the round of Africa, and doubled the Cape of Good Hope!"

"Who told you that she would make the round of Africa, and double the Cape of Good Hope, sir?"

"Well, unless the *Nautilus* sails on dry land, and passes above the isthmus — "

"Or beneath it, Professor."

"Beneath it?"

"Certainly," replied Captain Nemo, quietly. "A long time ago Nature made under this tongue of land what man has this day made on its surface."

"What! such a passage exists?"

"Yes; a subterranean passage, which I have named the Arabian tunnel. It takes us beneath Suez, and opens into the Gulf of Pelusium."

"But this isthmus, is it not composed of nothing but quicksands?"

"To a certain depth. But fifty-five yards down there is a solid layer of rock."

"Did you discover this passage by chance?" I asked, more and more surprised.

"Chance and reasoning, sir; and by reasoning even more than by chance. Not only does it exist, but I have used it several times. Without that I should not have ventured this day into the impassable Red Sea. I noticed that in the Red Sea and in the Mediterranean there exist a certain number of fishes that are perfectly identical. So I asked myself, was it possible that there was no communication between the two seas? If there was, the subterranean current must necessarily run from the Red Sea to the Mediterranean, because of the difference of level. I caught a large number of fishes in the neighborhood of Suez. I passed a copper ring through their tails, and threw them back into the sea. Some months later, on the coast of Syria, I caught some of my ringed fish. Thus the communication between the two was proved. I then sought for it with my *Nautilus;* I discovered it, ventured into it, and before long, sir, you too will have passed through my Arabian tunnel!"

From eight to nine o'clock the *Nautilus* remained some fathoms under the water. According to my calculation we must have been very near Suez. Through the panel of the salon I saw the bottom of the rocks brilliantly lit up by our electric lamp. We seemed to be leaving the straits behind.

At a quarter-past nine, the vessel having returned to the surface, I mounted the platform. Most impatient to pass through Captain Nemo's tunnel, I could not stay in one place, so I came to breathe in the fresh night air.

Soon in the shadow I saw a pale light, blurred by the fog, shining about a mile from us.

"A floating lighthouse!" said someone near me.

I turned, and saw the captain.

"It is the floating light of Suez," he continued. "It will not be long before we gain the entrance of the tunnel."

"The entrance cannot be easy?"

"No, sir; and for that reason I am accustomed to enter the steersman's cage and myself direct our course. And now if you will go down, Professor, the *Nautilus* is going under the waves, and will not return to the surface until we have passed through the Arabian tunnel."

Captain Nemo led me toward the central staircase. Halfway down he opened a door, crossed the upper deck, and landed in the pilot's cage, which it may be remembered rose at the end of the platform. It was a cabin measuring six feet square, very much like that occupied by the pilot on the steamboats of the Mississippi or Hudson. In the midst worked a wheel, placed vertically, and caught to the tiller rope, which ran to the back of the *Nautilus*. Four light ports with lenticular glasses, set in a groove in the partition of the cabin, allowed the man at the wheel to see in all directions.

This cabin was dark, but soon my eyes grew accustomed to it, and I perceived the pilot with his hands on the wheel. Outside, the sea was vividly lit by the lantern, which shed its rays from the back of the cabin to the other end of the platform.

"Now," said Captain Nemo, "let us try to make our passage."

Electric wires connected the pilot's cage with the machinery room, and from there the captain could control the direction and speed of the *Nautilus*. He pressed a metal knob, and at once the speed of the screw diminished.

I looked in silence at the high straight wall we were running by at this moment, the immovable base of a massive coast. We followed it thus for an hour.

At a quarter past ten, the captain himself took the helm. A large gallery, black and deep, opened before us. The *Nautilus* went boldly into it. A strange roaring was heard round its sides. It was the waters of the Red Sea, which the incline of the tunnel precipitated violently toward the Mediterranean. The *Nautilus* went with the torrent, rapid as an arrow.

On the walls of the narrow passage I could see nothing but brilliant rays, straight lines, furrows of fire, traced on the rock by the great speed and the brilliant electric light. My heart beat fast.

At thirty-five minutes past ten, Captain Nemo quitted the helm, and, turning to me, announced: "The Mediterranean!"

In less than twenty minutes, the *Nautilus*, carried along by the torrent, had passed through the Isthmus of Suez!

THE GRECIAN ARCHIPELAGO

THE NEXT DAY, the 12th of February, at the dawn of day, the *Nautilus* rose to the surface. I hastened onto the platform. Three miles to the south the dim outline of Pelusium was to be seen. We were in the other sea. About seven o'clock Ned and Conseil joined me.

"Well, Sir Naturalist," said the Canadian, in a slightly jovial tone, "and the Mediterranean?"

"We are floating on its surface, friend Ned."

"What!" said Conseil, "this very night!"

"Yes, this very night. In a few minutes we have passed under this impassable isthmus."

"I do not believe it," replied the Canadian.

"Then you are wrong, Master Land," I said. "This low coast which rounds off to the south is the Egyptian coast. And you, who have such good eyes, Ned, you can see the jetty of Port Said stretching into the sea."

The Canadian looked and exclaimed; "Certainly you are right, sir, and your captain is a first-rate man. We are in the Mediterranean. Good! Now, if you please, let us talk of our own little affair, but so that no one hears us."

I knew what the Canadian wanted, and I thought it better to let him talk, as he wished it. So we all three sat down near the lantern, where we were less exposed to the spray of the blades.

"Now, Ned, we listen; what have you to tell us?"

"What I have to tell you is very simple. We are in Europe; and before Captain Nemo's whims drag us once more to the bottom of the Polar Seas, or lead us into Oceania, I ask to leave the *Nautilus*."

I wished in no way to shackle the liberty of my companions, but I certainly felt no desire to leave Captain Nemo.

Thanks to him, and thanks to his *Nautilus*, I was each day nearer the completion of my submarine studies. And I was rewriting my book of submarine depths in its very element. Should I ever again have such an opportunity of observing the wonders of the ocean? No, certainly not! And I could not bring myself to the idea of abandoning the *Nautilus* before my investigations were completed.

"Friend Ned, answer me frankly, are you tired of being on board? Are you sorry that destiny has thrown us into Captain Nemo's hands?"

The Canadian remained some moments without answering. Then crossing his arms, he said, "Frankly, I do not regret this journey under the seas. I am glad to have made it. But now that it is made, let us have done with it."

"It will come to an end, Ned."

"Where and when?"

"Where I do not know — when I cannot say. Or rather, I suppose it will end when these seas have nothing more to teach us."

"Then what do you hope for?" demanded the Canadian.

"Where shall we be in six months, if you please, Sir Naturalist?"

"Perhaps in China. You know the *Nautilus* is a rapid traveler. It goes through water as swallows fly through the air, or as an express train on the land. It does not fear frequented

187

seas. Who can say that it may not beat the coasts of France, England, or America, to which flight may be attempted as advantageously as here."

"Professor," replied the Canadian, "your arguments are rotten at the core. You speak in the future. 'We shall be there! We shall be here!' I speak in the present: we *are* here, and we must profit by it."

Ned Land's logic pressed me hard, and I felt myself beaten on that ground. I knew not what argument to present in my favor.

"Sir," continued Ned, "let us suppose Captain Nemo should this day offer you your liberty. Would you accept it?"

"I do not know," I answered.

"And if," he added, "the offer he made you this day was never to be renewed, would you accept it?"

"Friend Ned, this is my answer. Your reasoning is against me. We must not rely on Captain Nemo's goodwill. Common caution forbids him to set us at liberty. On the other side, caution bids us profit by the first opportunity to leave the *Nautilus*."

"Well, Professor, that is wisely said."

"Only one observation — just one. The occasion must be serious, and our first attempt must succeed. If it fails, we shall never find another, and Captain Nemo will never forgive us."

"All that is true," replied the Canadian. "But your observation applies equally to all attempts at flight, whether in two years, or in two days. But the fact remains: if a favorable opportunity presents itself, it must be seized."

"Agreed! and now, Ned, will you tell me what you mean by a favorable opportunity?"

"It will be that which, on a dark night, brings the *Nautilus* a short distance from some European coast."

"And you will try and save yourself by swimming?"

"Yes, if we are near enough to the bank, and if the vessel is floating at that time. Not if the bank is far away, and the boat is under the water."

"And in that case?"

"In that case, I should seek to make myself master of the small boat. I know how it works. We must get inside, and the bolts once drawn, we shall come to the surface of the water, without even the pilot, who is in the bows, perceiving our flight."

"Well, Ned, watch for the opportunity; but do not forget that a hitch will ruin us."

"I will not forget, sir."

"And now, Ned, would you like to know what I think of your project?"

"Certainly, Professor."

"Well, I think — I do not say I hope — I think that this favorable opportunity will never present itself."

"Why not?"

"Because Captain Nemo cannot hide from himself that we have not given up all hope of regaining our liberty, and he will be on his guard, above all, in the seas, and in the sight of European coasts."

"We shall see," replied Ned Land, shaking his head determinedly.

"And now, Ned," I added, "let us stop here. Not another word on the subject. The day that you are ready, come and let us know, and we will follow you. I rely entirely upon you."

Thus ended a conversation which, at no very distant time, led to very grave results.

I must say here that facts seemed to confirm my foresight, to the Canadian's great despair. Did Captain Nemo distrust us in these frequented seas? Or did he only wish to hide himself from the numerous vessels of all nations which plowed the Mediterranean? I could not tell. But we were oftener under water, and far from the coast. And if the *Nau-*

tilus did emerge, nothing was to be seen but the pilot's cage. And sometimes the boat went to great depths.

The next day, the 14th of February, I resolved to spend some hours in studying the fishes of the Archipelago. But for some reason or other, the panels remained hermetically sealed. Upon taking the course of the *Nautilus* I found that we were heading toward the ancient Isle of Crete. At the time I embarked on the *Abraham Lincoln,* the whole of this island had risen in insurrection against the despotism of the Turks. But of how it had fared since, I was absolutely ignorant, and Captain Nemo, deprived of all land communications, could not tell me.

When that night I found myself alone with him in the salon, he seemed to be silent and preoccupied. Then, contrary to his custom, he ordered both panels to be opened, and going from one to the other, observed the waters attentively. Why, I could not guess; so I used my time in studying the fish passing before my eyes. My eyes were feasting on these wonders of the sea, when they were suddenly struck by an unexpected apparition.

In the midst of the waters a man appeared, a diver carrying at his belt a leathern purse. It was not a body abandoned to the waves. It was a living man, swimming with a strong hand, disappearing occasionally to take breath at the surface.

I turned toward Captain Nemo, and in an agitated voice exclaimed, "A man shipwrecked! He must be saved at any price!"

The captain did not answer me, but came and leaned against the panel.

The man had approached; and with his face flattened against the glass, was looking at us.

To my great amazement, Captain Nemo signed to him. The diver answered with his hand, mounted immediately to the surface of the water, and did not appear again.

"Do not be uncomfortable," said Captain Nemo. "It is Nicholas of Cape Matapan. He is well known in all the Cyclades. A bold diver! Water is his element, and he lives more in it than on land, going continually from one island to another, even as far as Crete."

Saying this, Captain Nemo went toward a piece of furniture standing near the left panel of the salon. Then I saw a chest made of iron, on the cover of which was a copper plate bearing the cipher of the *Nautilus* with its device.

At that moment, the Captain, without noticing my presence, opened a sort of strong box, which held many ingots.

They were ingots of gold. From whence came this precious metal, which represented an enormous sum? Where had the captain gathered it? And what was he going to do with it?

I did not say a word. I looked. Captain Nemo took the ingots one by one, and arranged them methodically in the chest, which he filled entirely. I estimated the contents at more than 4000 lbs., all gold!

The chest was then securely fastened, and the captain wrote an address on the lid, in modern Greek.

This done, Captain Nemo pressed a knob, the wire of which communicated with the quarters of the crew. Four men appeared, and, not without some trouble, pushed the chest out of the salon. Then I heard them hoisting it up the iron staircase by means of pulleys.

Captain Nemo turned to me.

"And you were saying, sir?" said he.

"I was saying nothing, Captain."

"Then, sir, if you will allow me, I will wish you good-night."

Whereupon he turned and left the salon.

I returned to my room, where I vainly tried to sleep. I sought the connecting link between the apparition of the diver and the chest filled with gold. Soon, I felt by certain movements of pitching and tossing, that the *Nautilus* was leaving the depths and returning to the surface.

Then I heard steps upon the platform! and I knew they were unfastening the small boat, and launching it upon the waves. For one instant it struck the side of the *Nautilus*, then all noise ceased.

Two hours later, I heard the same noise. The boat hoisted on board, replaced in its socket, and the *Nautilus* again plunged under the waves.

So these millions had been transported to their address. To what point of the continent? Who was Captain Nemo's correspondent?

The next day, I related to Conseil and the Canadian the events of the night, which had excited my curiosity to the highest degree. My companions were not less surprised than myself.

"But where does he take his millions to?" asked Ned Land.

To that there was no possible answer. I returned to the salon after having breakfast, and set to work. Till five o'clock in the evening, I was busy arranging my notes. But at five o'clock I felt so great a heat that I was obliged to take off my coat. It was strange, for we were not near the equator; and even then the *Nautilus*, submerged as it was, would experience no change of temperature. I looked at the manometer. It showed a depth of sixty feet, to which atmospheric heat could never attain.

I continued my work, but the temperature rose to such a pitch as to be intolerable.

"Could there be fire on board?" I asked myself.

I was leaving the salon, when Captain Nemo entered. He approached the thermometer, consulted it, and turning to me, said, "one hundred degrees."

"I have noticed it, Captain," I replied; "and if it gets much hotter we cannot bear it."

"Oh! sir, it will not get hotter if we do not wish it."

"You can reduce it as you please, then?"

"No; but I can go further from the stove which produces it."

"It is outward then!"

"Certainly. We are floating in a current of boiling water."

"Is it possible!" I exclaimed.

"Look."

The panels opened, and I saw the sea entirely white all round. A sulphurous smoke was curling amid the waves, which boiled like water in a copper. I placed my hand on one of the panes of glass, but the heat was so great that I quickly took it off again.

"Where are we?" I asked.

"Near the Island of Santorin, sir," replied the captain. "I wished to give you a sight of the curious spectacle of a submarine eruption."

"I thought," said I, "that the formation of these new islands was ended."

"Nothing is ever ended in the volcanic parts of the sea," replied Captain Nemo, "and the globe is always being worked by subterranean fires. You see I have marked the new islands."

I returned to the glass. The *Nautilus* was no longer moving, the heat was becoming unbearable. The sea, which until now had been white, was red, owing to the presence of salts of iron. In spite of the ship's being hermetically sealed, an insupportable smell of sulphur filled the salon, and the brilliancy of the electricity was entirely extinguished by bright scarlet flames. I was in a bath, I was choking, I was broiled.

"We can remain no longer in this boiling water," said I to the captain.

"It would not be wise," replied the impassive Captain Nemo.

An order was given. The *Nautilus* tacked about and left the furnace of heat. A quarter of an hour later we were breathing fresh air on the surface. The thought then struck me that, if Ned Land has chosen this part of the sea for our flight, we should never come out alive.

The next day, the 16th of February, we left the basin which, between Rhodes and Alexandria, is reckoned about 1500 fathoms in depth. The *Nautilus*, passing some distance from Cerigo, left the Grecian Archipelago, after having doubled Cape Matapan.

I saw no more of the interior of this Mediterranean than a traveler by express train sees of the landscape which flies before his eyes.

With regard to the species of fish common to the Atlantic and the Mediterranean, the giddy speed of the *Nautilus* prevented me from observing them with any degree of accuracy.

On the 18th day of February, about three o'clock in the morning, we were at the entrance of the Straits of Gibraltar. There once existed two currents: an upper one, long since recognized, which conveys the waters of the ocean into the basin of the Mediterranean;

and a lower counter-current, which reasoning has now shown to exist. Indeed, the volume of water in the Mediterranean, incessantly added to the waves of the Atlantic, and by rivers falling into it, would each year raise the level of this sea, for its evaporation is not sufficient to restore the equilibrium. As it is not so, we must necessarily admit the existence of an undercurrent, which empties into the basin of the Atlantic, through the Straits of Gibraltar, the surplus waters of the Mediterranean. A fact indeed, and it was this counter-current by which the *Nautilus* profited. It advanced rapidly by the narrow pass. For one instant I caught a glimpse of the beautiful ruins of the temple of Hercules, buried in the ground, according to Pliny, and with the low island which supports it; and a few minutes later we were floating on the Atlantic.

VIGO BAY

THE ATLANTIC! An ocean whose winding shores are watered by the largest rivers of the world — the St. Lawrence, the Mississippi, the Amazon, the Plata, the Orinoco, the Niger, the Senegal, the Elbe, the Loire and the Rhine — and which terminates in those two terrible points so dreaded by mariners, Cape Horn, and the Cape of Tempests!

The *Nautilus* was piercing the water with its sharp spur, after having accomplished nearly 10,000 leagues in three months and a half, a distance greater than the great circle of the earth. Where were we going now? And what was reserved for the future? The *Nau-*

tilus, leaving the Straits of Gibraltar, had gone far out. It returned to the surface of the waves, and our daily walks on the platform were restored to us.

I mounted at once, accompanied by Ned Land and Conseil. About twelve miles off, we could dimly see Cape St. Vincent, forming the southwestern point of the Spanish peninsula. A strong southerly gale was blowing. The sea was swollen and billowy, and the *Nautilus* rocked violently. It was almost impossible to keep one's footing on the platform, as the heavy rollers washed over it every instant. So, after inhaling some mouthfuls of fresh air, we descended.

I returned to my room, Conseil to his cabin. But the Canadian, with a preoccupied air, followed me. Our rapid passage across the Mediterranean had not allowed him to put his project into execution, and he could not help showing his disappointment. When the door of my room was shut, he sat down and looked at me silently.

"Friend Ned," said I, "I understand you. But you cannot reproach yourself. To have attempted to leave the *Nautilus* under the circumstances would have been folly."

Ned Land did not answer. His tightened

lips and frowning brow showed his state of mind.

"Let us see," I continued. "We need not despair yet. We are going up the coast of Portugal again, and France and England are not far off. We can easily find refuge. Now if the *Nautilus*, on leaving the Straits of Gibraltar, had turned south toward regions where there are no continents, I should share your uneasiness. But we know now that Captain Nemo does not shun civilized seas, and in a few days I think you can safely act."

Ned Land still looked at me fixedly. At length his lips parted, and he said, "It is for tonight."

I drew myself up suddenly. I was, I admit, little prepared for this communication. I wanted to answer the Canadian, but words would not come.

"We agreed to wait for an opportunity," continued Ned Land, "and the opportunity has arrived. This night we shall be but a few miles from the Spanish coast. It is cloudy. The wind blows freely. I have your word, Professor, and I rely upon you."

As I was still silent, the Canadian said, "Tonight, at nine o'clock. I have warned Conseil. At that moment, Captain Nemo will be in his room, probably in bed. Neither the engineers nor the ship's crew can see us. Conseil and I will gain the central staircase, and you, Professor, will remain in the library, two steps from us, awaiting my signal. The oars, the mast, and the sail are in the small boat. I have even succeeded in getting in some provisions. I have a wrench to unfasten the bolts which attach the small boat to the shell of the *Nautilus*. So all is ready — till tonight."

"The sea is bad."

"That I allow," replied the Canadian; "but we must risk that. Liberty is worth paying for. Besides, the boat is strong, and a few miles with a fair wind to carry us is no great thing. Who knows but by tomorrow we may be a hundred leagues away? Let circumstances only favor us, and by ten or eleven o'clock we shall have landed on some spot of *terra firma*, alive or dead."

With these words, the Canadian withdrew, leaving me almost dumb. I had imagined that, the chance gone, I should have time to reflect and discuss the matter. My obstinate companion had given me no time; and, after all, what could I have said to him? Ned Land was perfectly right. Tomorrow Captain Nemo might take us far from all land.

At that moment a rather loud hissing told me that the air tanks were filling, and that the *Nautilus* was sinking under the waves of the Atlantic.

A sad day I passed, between the desire of regaining my liberty, and of abandoning the wonderful *Nautilus*, and leaving my submarine studies incomplete.

Twice I went to the salon. I wished to consult the compass. I wished to see if the direction the *Nautilus* was taking was bringing us nearer or taking us farther from the coast. But, no — the *Nautilus* kept in Portuguese waters.

I must therefore prepare for flight. My luggage was not heavy — nothing more than my notes.

As to Captain Nemo, I asked myself what he would think of our escape — what trouble, what wrong it might cause him, and what he might do in case we failed. Certainly I had had no cause to complain of him as a host. On the contrary, never was hospitality freer than his. But in leaving him I could not be taxed with ingratitude. No oath bound us to him. It was on the strength of circumstances he relied, and not upon our word, to keep us forever.

Would chance bring me the captain's presence before our departure? I wished it, and I feared it at the same time. I listened for his steps in the room next to mine. No sound reached my ear. I felt an unbearable uneasiness. This day of waiting seemed to last for an eternity.

My dinner was served in my room as usual. I ate but little and left the table at seven o'clock. A hundred and twenty minutes separated me from the moment in which I was to join Ned Land. My agitation redoubled. My pulse beat violently. I could not remain quiet.

I wanted to see the salon for the last time. I descended the stairs to the museum where I had passed so many useful and agreeable hours. I looked again at all its riches, all its treasures, like a man on the eve of an eternal exile. These wonders of Nature, these masterpieces of art, amongst which, for so many days, my life had been concentrated, I was going to abandon forever!

I should have liked to take a last look through the windows of the salon into the waters of the Atlantic. But the panels were hermetically closed, and a cloak of steel separated me from that ocean which I had not yet explored.

In passing through the salon, I came near the door which opened into the captain's room. To my great surprise, this door stood ajar. I drew back, involuntarily. If Captain Nemo should be in his room, he could see me. But hearing no noise, I drew nearer. The room was deserted. I pushed open the door, and took some steps forward. Still the same monk-like severity of aspect.

Suddenly the clock struck eight. The first beat of the hammer on the bell startled me to action. I trembled as if an invisible eye had plunged into my most secret thoughts, and I hurried from the room.

There my eye fell upon the compass. Our course was still north. The log indicated moderate speed, the manometer a depth of about sixty feet.

I returned to my room, clothed myself warmly — sea boots, an otterskin cap and a great coat lined with sealskin. I was ready, I was waiting. The vibration of the screw alone broke the deep silence which reigned on board. I listened attentively. Would no loud voice suddenly inform me that Ned Land had been surprised in his projected flight? A mortal dread hung over me, and I vainly tried to regain my accustomed coolness.

At a few minutes to nine, I put my ear to the captain's door. No noise. I left my room and returned to the salon, which was dimly lit, but deserted.

I opened the door to the library. The same insufficient light, the same solitude. I stood near the door leading to the central staircase, and there waited for Ned Land's signal.

At that moment the trembling of the screw diminished, then it stopped entirely. The silence was now only disturbed by the beatings of my own heart. Suddenly a slight shock was felt. I knew that the *Nautilus* had stopped at the bottom of the ocean. My uneasiness increased. The Canadian's signal did not come. I felt inclined to join Ned Land and beg of him to put off his attempt. I felt that we were not sailing under our usual conditions.

At this moment the salon door opened, and Captain Nemo appeared. "Ah, sir!" he said, apparently not noticing my warm clothing. "I have been looking for you. Do you know the history of Spain?"

"Very slightly," I answered.

"Come, sit down," he said. "I will tell you a curious episode in this history."

"I listen, Captain," said I, not knowing

what he was driving at, and asking myself if this story would have any bearing on our projected flight.

"Sir, if you have no objection, we will go back to 1702. Your French king Louis XIV, thinking to bring the Pyrenees under his yoke, had imposed the Duke of Anjou, his grandson, on the Spaniards. This prince reigned under the name of Philip V, and had a strong party against him abroad. Indeed, the preceding year, the royal houses of Holland, Austria, and England had concluded a treaty of alliance. They intended to pluck the crown of Spain from the head of Philip V, and place it on that of an archduke.

"Spain must resist this coalition; but she was almost entirely unprovided with either soldiers or sailors. However, money would not fail them, provided that their galleons, laden with gold and silver from America, once entered their ports. And about the end of 1702 they expected a rich convoy. This convoy was to go to Cadiz, but the Admiral, hearing that an English fleet was cruising in those waters, resolved to make for a French port.

"The Spanish commanders of the convoy objected to this decision. They wanted to land at a Spanish port. If not Cadiz, then the port of Vigo, situated on the northwest coast of Spain. This port was not blocked. So the galleons entered Vigo Bay.

"Unfortunately, the bay was an open road which could not be defended from the sea. The ships must therefore be hastily unloaded before the arrival of the English fleet. But this is what passed:

"The merchants of Cadiz had the privilege of receiving all merchandise coming from the West Indies. Now to unload the treasure at Vigo was to deprive them of their rights. So the Cadiz merchants obtained an order from the weak-minded Philip that the convoy must remain in the bay until danger from the enemy was over, without discharging its precious cargo.

"But on the 22nd of October, 1702, the English vessels sailed into Vigo Bay. The Admiral fought bravely, but was losing. Rather than have the treasure fall into the enemy's hands, he burned and scuttled every galleon. They went to the bottom carrying their immense riches with them."

Captain Nemo stopped. I admit I could not yet see why this history should interest me.

"Well?" I asked.

"Well, Professor," replied Captain Nemo, "we are in that same Vigo Bay; and it rests with you whether you will penetrate its mysteries."

The captain rose, telling me to follow him. The salon was dark, but the panels had been opened. Through the transparent glass the waves were sparkling.

For half a mile around the *Nautilus*, the waters seemed bathed in electric light. The sandy bottom was clean and bright. Some of the ship's crew in their diving gear were clearing away half rotten barrels and empty cases from the midst of the blackened wrecks. From these cases and barrels escaped ingots of gold and silver, cascades of *piastres* and jewels. Sand was heaped up with them. Laden with their precious booty the men returned to the *Nautilus*, disposed of their burden, and went back to this inexhaustible fishery of gold and silver.

I understood now. This was the scene of the battle of October 22, 1702. Here on this very spot the galleons laden for the Spanish government had sunk. Here Captain Nemo came, according to his wants, to pack up those millions with which he burdened the *Nautilus*. It was for him and him alone that the New World had given up her precious metals. He was heir direct, without anyone to share, in those treasures torn from the Incas by their Spanish conquerors.

"Did you know, sir," he asked, smiling, "that the sea contained such riches?"

"I knew," I answered, "that they value the money held in these waters at two million."

"Doubtless. But to extract this money the expense would be greater than the profit. Here, on the contrary, I have but to pick up what man has lost — and not only in Vigo Bay, but in a thousand other spots where shipwrecks have happened, and which are marked on my submarine map. Can you understand now the source of the millions I am worth?

"And you think then, sir, that these riches are lost because I gather them? Is it for myself alone, that I take the trouble to collect these treasures? Do you think I am ignorant that there are suffering beings and oppressed races on this earth — victims to avenge? Do you not understand?"

Captain Nemo stopped at these last words, regretting perhaps that he had spoken so much. But I had guessed that whatever the motive was that had forced him to seek independence under the sea, it had left him still a man. His heart still beat for the sufferings of humanity, and his immense charity was for oppressed races as well as individuals. I then understood for whom those millions were destined, which were forwarded by Captain Nemo when the *Nautilus* was cruising in the waters of Crete.

A VANISHED CONTINENT

THE NEXT MORNING, the 19th of February, the
Canadian entered my room. He looked very
disappointed.

"Well, sir?" said he.

"Well, Ned, fortune was against us yester-
day."

"Yes. That captain stopped exactly at the
hour we intended leaving his vessel."

"Yes, Ned, he had business at his banker's."

"His banker's!"

"Or rather his banking-house. By that I
mean the ocean, where his riches are safer
than in the state treasuries."

I then related to the Canadian the incidents
of the preceding night, hoping to bring him

back to the idea of not abandoning the captain. But Ned only regretted that he had not been able to take a walk among the treasures of Vigo Bay on his own account.

"However," said he, "all is not ended. It is only a lost blow of the harpoon. Another time we will succeed; and tonight, if necessary. . . ."

"In what direction is the *Nautilus* headed?" I asked.

"I do not know," replied Ned.

"Well, we shall soon see."

The Canadian returned to Conseil. As soon as I was dressed, I went into the salon. The compass was not reassuring. The course of the *Nautilus* was S.S.W. We were turning our backs on Europe.

I waited with some impatience till the ship's place was located on the chart. At about half-past eleven our vessel rose to the ocean's surface. I rushed toward the platform. Ned Land had preceded me. No land in sight — nothing but an immense sea. The weather was cloudy and a gale was blowing up. Ned raved as he tried to pierce the cloudy horizon. He still hoped that behind all that fog stretched the land he so longed for. But as the sea became more billowy, we descended and the panel closed.

An hour later, upon consulting the chart,

I saw the position of the *Nautilus* was marked at 16° 17' long., and 33° 22' lat., at 150 leagues from the nearest coast. There was no means of flight, and I leave you to imagine Ned's rage when I informed him of our situation.

For myself, I was not particularly sorry. I felt lightened of the load which had oppressed me, and was able to return with some degree of calmness to my accustomed work.

That night, about eleven o'clock, I received a most unexpected visit from Captain Nemo. He asked me very graciously if I felt tired from my watch of the night before. I answered in the negative.

"Then, Professor, I propose a curious excursion. You have visited the submarine depths only by daylight, under the brightness of the sun. Would it suit you to see them in the darkness of the night?"

"Most willingly."

"I warn you, the way will be tiring. We shall have far to walk, and must climb a mountain. The way is rough."

"What you say, Captain, only heightens my curiosity. I am ready to follow you."

"Come then, sir, we will put on our diving gear."

Arrived at the robing room, I saw that

neither of my companions nor any of the ship's crew were to follow us on this excursion.

In a few moments we had put on our diving gear. On our backs were tanks abundantly filled with air, but no electric lamps were prepared. I called the captain's attention to the fact.

"They will be useless," he replied.

I thought I had not heard right, but I could not repeat my observation, for the captain's head had already disappeared in the metal case. I finished harnessing myself, I felt them put an iron-pointed stick into my hand, and some minutes later we set foot on the bottom of the Atlantic. Midnight was near. The waters were profoundly dark, but Captain Nemo pointed out in the distance a reddish spot, a sort of large light shining brilliantly, about two miles from the *Nautilus*. What this fire might be, what could feed it, why and how it lit up the ocean depths, I could not say. In any case, it did light our way — vaguely, it is true — but I soon accustomed myself to the peculiar darkness, and I understood, under such circumstances, the uselessness of lamps.

As we advanced, I heard a kind of pattering above my head. I soon understood the cause. It was rain falling violently, and crisping the surface of the waves. Instinctively the thought flashed across my mind that I should be wet through! By the water! In the midst of the water! I could not help laughing at the odd idea.

After half an hour's walk the bottom became stony, and the water slightly phosphorescent. I caught a glimpse of stones covered with millions of zoophytes, and masses of seaweed. My feet often slipped upon this carpet of seaweed, and without my iron-tipped stick I should have fallen more than once. In turning round, I could still see the whitish lantern of the *Nautilus* beginning to pale in the distance.

But the rosy light which guided us increased and lit up the horizon. The presence of this fire under water puzzled me. Was it some electric outpouring? Was I going toward a natural phenomenon as yet unknown to the scientists of the earth? Or even, more wondrous still, had the hand of man fanned this flame? Was I to meet in these depths companions and friends of Captain Nemo whom he was going to visit, and who, like him, led this strange existence? Should I find down there a whole colony of exiles, weary of the miseries of this earth, who had sought and found independence in the deep ocean? All these foolish and unreasonable ideas pursued me. And in this condition of mind, over-excited by the succession of wonders continually passing before my eyes, I should not have been surprised to meet at the bottom of the sea one of those submarine towns of which Captain Nemo dreamed.

Our way grew steadily brighter. The glimmer came in rays from the summit of a mountain about 800 feet high. But what I saw was simply a reflection, developed by the clearness of the waters. The source of this strange light was a fire on the opposite side of a mountain.

In the midst of this stony maze, furrowing the bottom of the Atlantic, Captain Nemo advanced without hesitation. He knew this terrain. Doubtless he had often traveled over it, and I followed him with unshaken confidence. He seemed to me like a genie of the sea. And, as he walked before me, I could not help admiring his stature, black against the luminous horizon.

It was one o'clock in the morning when we reached the first slopes of the mountain. But to get to it we must venture through a vast forest.

Yes, a forest of dead trees without leaves, without sap — trees petrified by the action of the water. Picture to yourself a mountain forest — but swallowed up in water. The paths were nearly blocked with seaweed and a whole world of crustacea. I went along, climbing the rocks, striding over extended trunks, breaking sea vines which hung from one tree to the other, and frightening the fishes, which "flew" from branch to branch!

Two hours after quitting the *Nautilus*, we had crossed the line of trees. A hundred feet above our heads rose the top of the mountain, which cast a shadow on the brilliant light of the opposite slope. Petrified shrubs rose fantastically here and there.

Massive rocks had split and formed deep grottoes and unfathomable holes where unknown creatures lived. My blood curdled when I saw enormous antennae blocking my way, or some frightful claw closing in the shadow of some cavity. Millions of luminous spots shone brightly in the midst of the darkness. They were the eyes of giant crustacea crouched in their holes. Giant lobsters moving their claws with the clicking sound of pincers, titanic crabs, and frightful looking monsters, that wove their tenacles like a living nest of serpents.

We had now arrived on the first level, where other surprises awaited me. Before us lay some picturesque ruins, which revealed the hand of man! There were vast heaps of stone, where stood vague and shadowy forms of castles and temples, all clothed with blossoming zoophytes. Over them, instead of ivy, seaweed threw a thick cloak. But what was this portion of the globe? Who had fashioned those rocky structures? Where had Captain Nemo's fancy hurried me?

Unable to ask him because of the helmets we wore, I stopped him by seizing his arm. But he shook his head. Pointing to the highest point of the mountain, he seemed to say:

"Come, come along! Come higher!"

I followed, and in a few minutes we had reached the top.

I looked down. The side we had just climbed did not rise more than seven or eight hundred feet above the level of the plain. But I saw that the opposite side of the mountain commanded from twice that height this part of the Atlantic Ocean floor. My eyes ranged far and wide, for the entire area was lit by a violent eruption. In fact, the mountain was a volcano!

Beyond the peak, in the midst of a rain of stones and scoriae, we could see a large crater vomiting forth torrents of molten lava which fell in a brilliant cascade down through the water. This volcano lit the lower plain like an immense torch, even to the extreme limits of the horizon. I said that the submarine crater threw up lava, but there were no flames. Flames require the oxygen of the air to feed upon, and cannot be developed under water. But the streams of molten lava glowed red and white with heat and slid to the bottom of the mountain like an eruption of Vesuvius.

There, indeed, under my eyes, ruined, destroyed, lay a town — its roofs open to the sky, its temples fallen, its arches dislocated, its columns lying on the ground. Yet in all the ruin one could still recognize massive Tuscan architecture. Farther on were some remains of a gigantic aqueduct, the high base of an Acropolis, with the floating outline of a Parthenon. There were traces of an ancient port, which had sunk with all its merchant vessels and its war galleys. Farther on, one could see long lines of sunken walls and broad deserted streets — a perfect Pompeii beneath the waters. Such was the sight that Captain Nemo brought before my eyes!

Where was I? I must know, at any cost. I tried again to communicate, but Captain Nemo stopped me by a gesture. Picking up a piece of chalk stone, he went to a rock of black basalt, and traced the one word:

ATLANTIS.

What a light shot through my mind! Atlantis, the ancient lost continent!

It was there now before my eyes, bearing eloquent testimony to the nature of its catastrophe. Here, *in fact,* was the lost continent of Atlantis, which modern historians thought was just an ancient legend! These drowned regions beyond the pillars of Hercules had been the home of the Atlantides, a rich and powerful people of ancient times, until a terrible fate overtook them.

Now, led by the strangest destiny, I was walking on the very spot where the first civilizations had walked!

While I was trying to fix in my mind every detail, Captain Nemo remained motionless, leaning against a rock. Was he dreaming of those generations long since disappeared? Was he asking them the secret of human destiny? Was it here this strange man came to steep himself in historical recollections, and live again this ancient life — he who wanted no modern one? What would I not have given to know his thoughts, to share them, to understand them! We remained for an hour at this place, contemplating the vast plain under the brightness of the lava, which was sometimes wonderfully intense. Rapid tremblings ran along the mountains caused by internal explosions.

At this moment the moon shone through the waters, and threw her pale rays on the buried continent. It was but a gleam, but what an indescribable effect!

At length the captain rose, cast one last look on the immense plain, and then bade me follow him.

We descended the mountain rapidly. Once past the forest, I saw the lantern of the *Nautilus* shining like a star. The captain walked straight to it, and we got on board as the first rays of light whitened the surface of the ocean.

THE SUBMARINE COAL-MINES

T HE NEXT DAY, the 20th of February, I awoke very late; it was eleven o'clock. I dressed quickly, and hastened to check the course of the *Nautilus*. The instruments showed it to be still toward the south, with a speed of twenty miles an hour, at a depth of fifty fathoms.

The species of fishes here did not vary much from those already noted. There were giant rays, fifteen feet broad, whose great muscular strength enabled them to shoot above the waves. There were sharks of many kinds, among them a gray shark fifteen feet long, with triangular sharp teeth, whose transparency rendered it almost invisible in the water.

About four o'clock, I saw the southerly horizon blocked by a high wall which seemed to close all exit. Its summit evidently passed the level of the ocean. It must be a continent, or at least an island — one of the Canaries, or of the Cape Verde Islands. I was ignorant of our exact position. In any case, such a wall seemed to me to mark the limits of that Atlantis, of which we had in reality passed over only the smallest part.

Much longer should I have remained at the window, admiring the beauties of sea and sky, but the panels closed. At this moment the *Nautilus* reached the side of this high wall. What would happen now I could not guess, but we no longer moved.

I returned to my room and lay down with the full intention of waking after a few hours' sleep. But it was eight o'clock the next day when I entered the salon. I looked at the manometer. It told me that the *Nautilus* was floating on the surface of the ocean. Then I heard steps on the platform.

I went to the panel. It was open; but, instead of broad daylight, as I expected, I was surrounded by profound darkness. Where were we? Was I mistaken? Was it still night? No; not a star was shining, and night has not that utter darkness.

I knew not what to think, when a voice near me said:

"Is that you, Professor?"

"Ah! Captain," I answered, "where are we?"

"Underground, sir."

"Underground!" I exclaimed. "And yet the *Nautilus* is floating on the surface? I do not understand."

"Wait a few minutes. Our lantern will be lit, and if you like light places, you will be satisfied."

So I stood on the platform and waited. The darkness was so complete that I could not even see Captain Nemo. But looking up, I seemed to catch a faint gleam, a kind of twilight filling a circular hole. At this instant the lantern was lit, and its vividness dispelled the dark. I closed my dazzled eyes for an instant, and then looked again. The *Nautilus* was stationary, floating near a mountain which formed a sort of harbor. The water supporting it, then, was a lake imprisoned by a circle of walls. I estimated that it was two miles in diameter and six in circumference. Its level — the manometer showed — could only be the same as the outside level, for there must necessarily be a connection between the lake and the sea. The high partitions, leaning forward on their base, grew into a vaulted roof bearing the shape of an immense funnel turned upside down, about five or six hundred yards in height. At the summit was a circular opening, by which I had caught the slight gleam of light, evidently daylight.

"Where are we?" I asked.

"In the very heart of an extinct volcano. Its interior was invaded by the sea after some great convulsion of the earth. While you were sleeping, Professor, the *Nautilus* penetrated this lagoon by a natural canal, which runs about ten yards beneath the surface of the ocean. This is our harbor of refuge — large, mysterious and sheltered from all gales. Show me, if you can, on the coasts of any of your continents or islands, another place that can give us such perfect refuge from all storms."

"Certainly," I replied, "you are in safety here, Captain Nemo. Who could reach you in the heart of a volcano? But did I not see an opening at its summit?"

"Yes. Its open crater, once filled with lava, now gives entrance to the life-giving air we breathe."

"But what is this volcanic mountain?"

"It belongs to one of the numerous islands with which this sea is strewn. To ships, it is simply an extinct volcano. To us it is an immense cavern. Chance led me to discover it, and chance has served me well."

"But of what use is this refuge, Captain? The *Nautilus* needs no port."

"No, sir. But it needs electricity to make it move, and the wherewithal to make that electricity — sodium to feed the elements, coal from which to get the sodium, and a coal mine to supply the coal. And exactly on this spot the sea covers entire forests embedded during the geological periods, which are now mineralized and transformed into coal. For me they are an inexhaustible mine."

"Your men follow the trade of miners here, then, Captain?"

"Exactly so. These mines extend under the waves like the mines of Newcastle. Here, in their diving suits, pickaxe and shovel in hand, my men extract the coal. When I burn it for the manufacture of sodium, the smoke, escaping from the center of the mountain, gives it the appearance of a still active volcano."

"And we shall see your companions at work?"

227

"No, not this time at least, for I am in a hurry to continue our submarine tour of the earth. So I shall content myself with drawing from the reserve of sodium I already possess. The time for loading is one day only, and then we continue our voyage. So if you wish to go over the cavern, and make the round of the lagoon, you must take advantage of today, Professor."

I thanked the captain, and went to look for my companions, who had not yet left their cabin. I invited them to follow me without telling them where we were. They mounted the platform. Conseil, who was astonished at nothing, seemed to look upon it as quite natural that he should wake under a mountain, after having fallen asleep under the waves. But Ned Land thought of nothing but finding whether the cavern had any exit. After breakfast, about ten o'clock, we set out to explore the mountain.

"Here we are, once more on land," said Conseil.

"I do not call this land," said the Canadian. "And besides, we are not on it, but beneath it."

Between the walls of the mountain and the waters of the lake lay a sandy shore, which,

at its greatest breadth, measured 500 feet.
On this soil one might easily make the tour
of the lake. But the base of the high partitions was stony ground, with volcanic blocks
and enormous pumice stones lying in heaps.
All these detached rock masses, polished in
the fires of the extinct volcano, shone resplen-
dent in the light of our electric lantern. The
mica dust from the shore, rising under our
feet, flew like a cloud of sparks. The ground
sloped upward and we soon reached the
steeper wall of the mountain. But we were
obliged to walk carefully, as our feet slipped
on crystal, feldspar, and quartz.

The volcanic nature of this enormous ex-
cavation was confirmed on all sides, and I
pointed it out to my companions.

"Picture to yourselves," said I, "this crater
filled with boiling lava that quickly rose up
through the opening of the mountain."

"I can picture it perfectly," said Conseil.
"But, sir, how is it that the one-time furnace
is replaced by the quiet waters of the lake?"

"Most probably, Conseil, because some convulsion beneath the ocean produced that very
opening which has served as a passage for
the *Nautilus*. Then the waters of the Atlantic
rushed into the interior of the mountain. But

many ages have passed since then, and the submerged volcano is now a peaceable grotto."

"Very well," replied Ned Land; "I accept the explanation, sir; but, in our own interests, I regret that the opening of the canal was not made above the level of the sea."

"But, friend Ned," said Conseil, "if the passage had not been under the sea, the *Nautilus* could not have gone through it."

We continued our climb, which became more and more perpendicular. Deep excavations, which we were obliged to cross, cut them here and there, and sloping masses that had to be gone around. We slid to our knees and crawled along. But Conseil's dexterity and the Canadian's strength surmounted all obstacles. At a height of about thirty-one feet, the nature of the ground changed.

We had now reached the upper crater where a more powerful light shone through. It shed a vague glimmer over these volcanic depressions forever buried in the bosom of this extinguished volcano. But our upward march was soon stopped. At a height of about 250 feet there were impassable obstacles. There was a complete vaulted arch overhanging us, and our ascent was changed to a circular walk. Some shrubs, and even some trees, grew from fractures in the walls. Between the streams of hardened lava, I saw some little violets growing. I smelled them with delight.

We had arrived at the foot of some sturdy dragon trees, which had pushed aside the rocks with their strong roots, when Ned Land exclaimed, "Ah! sir, a hive! a hive!"

"A hive!" I replied, with a gesture of incredulity.

"Yes, a hive," repeated the Canadian, "and bees humming round it."

I approached, and was bound to believe my own eyes. There, at a hole bored in one of the dragon trees, were some thousands of these ingenious insects, so common in all the Canaries, and whose produce is so much esteemed. Naturally enough, the Canadian wished to gather the honey, and I could not well oppose his wish. A quantity of dry leaves, mixed with sulphur, he lit with a spark from his flint, and he began to smoke out the bees. The humming ceased by degrees, and the hive eventually yielded several pounds of the sweetest honey, with which Ned Land filled his haversack.

"When I have mixed this honey with the paste of the breadfruit," said he, "I shall be able to offer you a wonderful cake."

"Upon my word," said Conseil, "it will be gingerbread."

"Never mind the gingerbread," said I. "Let us continue our interesting walk."

At every turn of the path we were following, we could view the lake below in all its length and breadth. The lantern lit up the whole of its peaceable surface. The *Nautilus* remained perfectly immovable. On the platform, and on the mountain, the ship's crew were working like black figures clearly silhouetted against the luminous atmosphere. We were now going round the highest crest of the first layers of rock which upheld the roof. Above us the crater seemed to gape like the mouth of a well. From this place the sky could be clearly seen, and clouds, dissipated by the west wind, leaving behind them, even on the summit of the mountain, their misty remnants — certain proof that they were only moderately high, for the volcano did not rise more than eight hundred feet above the level of the ocean.

Three quarters of an hour later, we had finished our roundabout walk, and were back on board the boat. The crew had just finished loading the sodium, and the *Nautilus* could have left that instant. But Captain Nemo gave no order. Did he wish to wait until night, and leave the submarine passage secretly? Perhaps so. Whatever it might be, the next day, the *Nautilus*, having left its port, steered clear of all land at a few yards beneath the waves of the Atlantic.

THE SARGASSO SEA AND SOUTHWARD

T HAT DAY the *Nautilus* crossed a singular part of the Atlantic Ocean — the Gulf Stream. Before it enters the Gulf of Mexico, at about 45° N. lat., this current divides into two arms, the principal one going toward the coast of Ireland and Norway, while the second bends to the south, on a line with the Azores. Then, touching the African shore, and describing a lengthened oval, the stream returns to the Antilles. This second arm — it is rather a collar than an arm — surrounds with its circles of warm water that portion of the cold, quiet, immovable ocean called the Sargasso Sea, a perfect lake in the open Atlantic. It takes no less than three years for the great current to pass round it.

Such was the region the *Nautilus* was now visiting — a perfect meadow, a close carpet of seaweed and tropical berries, so thick and so compact, that the stem of a vessel could hardly tear its way through it. And Captain Nemo, not wishing to entangle the propellers in this mass, kept some yards beneath the surface of the waves. The name Sargasso comes from the Spanish word "sargazzo," which means kelp. This kelp, or berry-plant, is the principal formation of this immense bank.

I was able to study the phenomenon in the very midst, where vessels rarely penetrate. Above us floated products of all kinds, heaped up among these brownish plants: trunks of trees; numerous wrecks, remains of keels, or ships' bottoms, side planks stove in and so weighted with shells and barnacles that they could not again rise to the surface. In time these substances, thus accumulated for ages, may become petrified by the action of the water, and will then form inexhaustible coal mines — a precious reserve prepared by far-seeing Nature for the moment when men shall have exhausted the mines of continents.

In the midst of this inextricable mass of

plants and seaweed, were charming tints of pink, green, red, blue and violet.

All the day of the 22nd of February we passed in the Sargasso Sea, where such fish as are partial to marine plants find abundant nourishment. The next day the ocean had returned to its accustomed aspect. From this time for nineteen days, from the 23rd of February to the 12th of March, the *Nautilus* kept to the middle of the Atlantic, carrying us at a constant speed. Captain Nemo evidently intended to complete his submarine tour of the world, and I imagined that he intended, after doubling Cape Horn, to return to the Australian seas of the Pacific.

Ned Land had cause for fear. In the large seas, empty of islands, we could not attempt to leave the boat.

The nineteen days mentioned above were uneventful. I saw little of the captain; he was at work. In the library I often found his books left open, especially those on natural history. My own work on submarine depths was covered with marginal notes, often contradicting my theories and systems. But it was very rare for him to discuss it with me. Sometimes I heard the melancholy tones of the organ, but only at night when the *Nautilus* moved upon the deserted ocean.

During this part of our voyage we sailed whole days on the surface of the waves. The sea seemed abandoned. A few sailing vessels were making for the Cape of Good Hope. One day we were followed by the boats of a whaler, who, no doubt, took us for some enormous whale of great price. But Captain Nemo did not wish the worthy fellows to lose their time and trouble, and ended the chase by plunging under the water.

Our navigation continued, and by the 13th of March, we had made about 13,000 leagues since our departure from the Pacific.

About eight o'clock on the morning of March 16th, the *Nautilus*, following the fifty-fifth meridian, cut the antarctic polar circle. Ice surrounded us on all sides, and closed the horizon. But Captain Nemo went from one opening to another. I cannot express my astonishment at the beauties of these new regions. The ice took most surprising forms. Here the grouping formed an oriental town, with mosques and minarets. There, a fallen city thrown to the earth, as it were, by some convulsion of Nature. The whole aspect was constantly changed by the oblique rays of the sun, or lost in the grayish fog amidst hurricanes of snow.

Often, seeing no exit, I thought we were prisoners. But then Captain Nemo would discover a new pass. He was never mistaken when he saw the thin threads of bluish water trickling along the ice-fields, and I had no doubt that he had already ventured into the midst of these antarctic seas before.

On the 16th of March, however, the ice-fields seemed to absolutely block our way. But Captain Nemo forced the *Nautilus* against it with frightful violence. The boat entered the brittle mass like a wedge, and split it with frightful cracklings. It was the battering ram of the ancients hurled by infinite strength. The ice, thrown high in the air, fell like hail around us.

Now the temperature was always at five degrees below zero. Every outward part of the *Nautilus* was covered with ice. A sailing vessel could never have worked its way through; only a vessel without sails and with electricity for power, could brave such conditions. At length, on the 18th of March, after many useless assaults, the *Nautilus* was finally blocked. It was no longer either streams, packs, or ice-fields, but an endless barrier, formed by ice mountains.

Under the spur of the *Nautilus* lay stretched a vast plain, entangled with confused blocks.

Here and there were sharp points and slender needles rising to a height of 200 feet. Farther on lay a steep shore clothed with grayish tints — huge mirrors reflecting a few rays of sunshine that were half drowned in fog. And over this desolate face of Nature a stern silence reigned, scarcely broken by the flapping of wings of petrels and puffins. Everything was frozen — even sound.

The captain had been observing our situation for some time past, when he said to me, "Well, sir, what do you think of this?"

"I think that we are caught, Captain."

"So, Professor, you really think that the *Nautilus* cannot disengage itself?" he asked.

"With difficulty, Captain. The season is already too far advanced for you to reckon on the breaking up of the ice."

"Ah! sir," said Captain Nemo, in an ironical tone, "you will always be the same. You see nothing but difficulties and obstacles. I say that not only can the *Nautilus* disengage itself, but also that it can go farther still."

"Farther to the south?" I asked, looking at the captain.

"Yes," replied the captain, coldly, "to the antarctic pole. . . . *You* know that I can do as I please with the *Nautilus!*"

Yes, I knew that. I knew that this man was

bold, even to rashness. But to conquer those obstacles which bristled round the South Pole, rendering it more inaccessible than the North (and even that had not yet been reached by the boldest navigators), was it not a mad enterprise which only a maniac would attempt? It then came into my head to ask Captain Nemo if he had ever explored the South Pole which, as far as the world knew, had never yet been trodden by a human creature.

"No, sir," he replied, "but we will discover it together. Where others have failed, *I* will not fail. I have never yet led my *Nautilus* so far into southern seas. But, I repeat, it shall go farther yet."

"I can well believe you, Captain," said I, in a slightly ironical tone. "I believe you! Let us go ahead! There are no obstacles for us! Let us smash this ice mountain! Let us blow it up! And if it resists, let us give the *Nautilus* wings to fly over it!"

"Over it, sir?" asked Captain Nemo quietly. "No, not *over* it, but *under* it!"

"Under it!" I exclaimed, a sudden idea of the captain's projects flashing upon my mind. I understood — the wonderful qualities of the *Nautilus* were going to serve us in this superhuman enterprise.

"For one foot of ice above the sea there are nine below it," Captain Nemo said. "If these ice mountains are 150 feet above the surface, they are 1000 feet beneath. And what is 1000 feet to the *Nautilus*?"

"Nothing, sir."

"The only difficulty," continued Captain Nemo, "is that of remaining several days without renewing our provision of air."

"Is that all? The *Nautilus* has vast air tanks. We can fill them, and they will supply us with all the oxygen we want."

"Well thought of," replied the captain, smiling. "But not wishing you to accuse me of rashness, I will first tell you of the obstacles. It is possible, if the sea exists at the South Pole, that it may be frozen to such a depth that we shall be unable to push our way to the surface."

"Captain," I said, "why should we not find the sea open at the South Pole as well as at the North? Until it is proved to the contrary, we may suppose either a continent or an ocean free from ice at these two points of the globe."

"I think so, too, Professor," replied Captain Nemo. "I only wish you to observe that, after having made so many objections to my project, you are now crushing me with arguments in its favor!"

The preparations for this daring attempt now began. The powerful pumps of the *Nautilus* were storing air in the tanks at high pressure. About four o'clock Captain Nemo announced the closing of the panels on the platform. I threw one last look at the massive mountain of ice which we were going to pass under. The weather was clear, the atmosphere was pure in this cold temperature — twelve degrees below zero. But the wind was down, and so the temperature was not unbearable. About ten men, armed with pickaxes, mounted the sides of the *Nautilus* to break the boat free of the ice around it. This operation was quickly performed, for the fresh ice was still very thin. We all went below. The water tanks were filled, and the *Nautilus* soon descended. I took my place with Conseil in the salon. Through the open panels we could see the lower beds of the Southern Ocean. At about 1000 feet, as Captain Nemo had foreseen, we were floating beneath the iceberg. But the *Nautilus* went lower still — it went to the depth of 400 fathoms.

In this open water, the *Nautilus* maintained a speed of twenty-six knots. If that was kept up, in forty hours we should reach the Pole.

The next morning, the 19th of March, I took my post once more in the salon. The log told me that the speed of the *Nautilus* had been slackened. It was then headed toward the surface, emptying its tanks very slowly. My heart beat fast. Were we going to emerge and regain the open sea? No! A shock told me that the *Nautilus* had struck the bottom of the iceberg, still very thick, judging from the deadened sound. We had indeed "struck," to use a sea expression, but at a thousand feet deep. This meant there were more than a thousand feet of ice above us; over 150 feet of it above the waterline.

Several times that day the *Nautilus* tried again, and every time it struck the ice, which lay like a ceiling above it. Sometimes the ice was 2000 feet in depth, and 300 feet above the surface. This was more than twice the height of the ice where the *Nautilus* had gone under the waves.

I carefully noted the different depths, and thus obtained a submarine profile of the ice mountain chain. That night we calculated that the ice was still between four and five hundred yards in depth. It was evidently diminishing, but what a thickness between us and the surface of the ocean! It was then eight. According to the daily custom on board the *Nautilus*, air should have been renewed four hours ago. As yet I did not suffer much, and Captain Nemo had not made any demand upon his reserve of oxygen.

My sleep was painful that night; hope and fear beseiged me. About three in the morning, I noticed that the lower surface of the iceberg was only about 50 feet deep. The ice barrier was by degrees becoming an ice-field, the mountain a plain.

My eyes never left the manometer. We were still rising diagonally to the surface, which sparkled in the electric rays of the *Nautilus*. The barrier was beginning to slope upward in the water. Mile after mile it grew steadily thinner. Finally, at six in the morning of that memorable day, the 20th of March, the door of the salon opened, and Captain Nemo appeared.

"The sea is open!" was all he said.

THE SOUTH POLE

I RUSHED onto the platform. Yes! It was the open sea — with but a few scattered ice floes and floating icebergs — a long stretch of sea. There were swarms of birds fluttering in the air, and myriads of fish in those waters, that ranged from light blue to deep green, according to the varying depths. The thermometer registered thirty-seven degrees above zero. It was comparative spring to us shut up as we had been behind the ice barrier, whose lengthened mass we could dimly see on our northern horizon.

"Are we at the Pole?" I asked the captain, with a beating heart.

"I do not know," he replied. "At noon I will take our bearing and we shall see."

"But will the sun break through this fog?" I asked, looking at the leaden sky.

"However little it shines, it will be enough for our purpose," replied the captain.

About ten miles south, a solitary island rose to a height of about 300 feet. We made for it, but carefully, for these waters were full of shoals. A narrow channel separated the island from a considerable stretch of land — perhaps a continent — for we could not see its limits.

The *Nautilus*, for fear of running aground, stopped about three cables' length from shore, and the small boat was launched. The captain, with two of his men carrying instruments, and Conseil and myself were in it. It was ten in the morning. I had not seen Ned Land.

"Sir," said I to Captain Nemo, "to you belongs the honor of being the first to set foot on this land."

"Yes, sir," said the captain; "and I do not hesitate to tread this South Pole because, up to this time, no human being has left a trace here."

Saying this he leaped lightly onto the sand. He climbed to a little promontory, and there, with his arms crossed, mute and motionless and with an eager look, he seemed to take possession of these southern regions. Then he turned to me:

"Whenever you like, sir."

I landed, followed by Conseil, leaving the two men in the boat. For some distance we walked over ground strewn with rubble — crushed reddish stone, cinders, and chunks of black lava and pumice stone. One could not mistake the volcanic origin of this island. In some parts, slight curls of smoke emitted a sulphurous smell, proving that the internal fires were still very active under the surface.

The fog did not lift, and at eleven we had not yet seen the sun. Its absence made me uneasy. Without it we could make no observations to determine whether we had reached the Pole.

When I rejoined Captain Nemo, I found him silently watching the sky. He seemed impatient and vexed. Not even this rash and powerful man could command the sun as he did the sea!

Noon came, and still no sun. We could not even guess its position behind the curtain of fog, and soon the fog turned to snow.

"Till tomorrow," said the captain quietly, and we returned to the *Nautilus*.

The snow continued till the next day, then ceased, and it became much colder. In the morning the fog seemed to lift, but the sun did not appear. If it did not shine on the morrow we would have to give it up. For the next day would be the equinox. After that, the sun would disappear behind the horizon for six months and the long polar night would begin. The next day the 21st of March at five in the morning, I mounted the platform. I found Captain Nemo there.

"The weather is lightening a little," said he. "I have some hope. After breakfast we will go on shore, and choose a post for observation."

That settled, I sought Ned Land. I wanted to take him with me. But the obstinate Canadian refused, and I saw that his bad humor grew day by day in this inaccessible place. I was not sorry for his refusal to go on land, under the circumstances. There were too many seals on shore. I felt we ought not to lay such temptations in this unreflecting fisherman's way.

As soon as breakfast was over, we went on

shore. The *Nautilus* had gone some miles farther up in the night, to a point on the coast where a sharp peak rose 1500 feet above the sea.

Besides me, the small boat took Captain Nemo, two men of the crew, and the instruments — a chronometer, a telescope, and a barometer. As we rowed toward shore I saw numerous whales: the right whale, the humpback and the finback among them. They were sporting in the quiet waters, safe from hunters.

At nine we landed. The sky was brightening as the fog lifted from the cold surface of the waters. Captain Nemo went toward the peak, which he doubtless meant to be his observatory. It was a painful ascent over the sharp chunks of lava and pumice, in an atmosphere often filled with a sulphurous smell from the smoking cracks. For a man unaccustomed to walk on land, the captain climbed the steep slopes with amazing agility.

It took us two hours to get to the summit of this rocky peak. Once there, we looked out over a vast sea. At our feet lay fields of dazzling whiteness, and over our heads a most welcome azure sky, free from fog. To the north we saw the disc of the sun like a ball of white-hot fire. Below us, spouting water-jets into the air, and in the distance lay the *Nautilus*, like a huge cetacean herself, asleep on the water.

At a quarter to twelve, the sun, then seen only by refraction, was shedding its last rays upon this deserted region. Captain Nemo marked the lengthening diagonal of its course from our position to the horizon. I held the chronometer. My heart beat fast. If the half-disc of the disappearing sun coincided with twelve o'clock on the chronometer, we were at the Pole itself.

"Twelve!" I exclaimed.

"The South Pole!" replied Captain Nemo, in a grave voice, handing me the glass, through which I saw the sun's orb cut in exactly equal parts by the horizon.

I looked at the last rays crowning the peak, and the shadows lengthening on the slopes. At that moment Captain Nemo, rested with his hand on my shoulder, said, "I, Captain Nemo, on this 21st day of March, 1868, have reached the South Pole on the ninetieth degree. And I take possession of this part of the globe, equal to one sixth of the know continents."

"In whose name, Captain?"

"In my own, sir!"

Saying which, Captain Nemo unfurled a black banner, bearing an N in gold. Then he turned toward the orb of day, whose last rays lapped the horizon of the sea, and exclaimed, "Farewell, sun! Disappear, thou radiant orb, and let the night of six months spread its shadows over my new domains!"

ACCIDENT OR INCIDENT

THE NEXT DAY, the 22nd of March, at six in the morning, we began preparations for departure. I say "day," but the last gleams of twilight were fading into the six-month long polar night.

When the tanks were filled with the supplies of air and water which we needed for our long trip under the ice, the *Nautilus* slowly descended to one thousand feet. Then the screw beat the water and we headed due north, at a speed of fifteen knots. Toward night the *Nautilus* was already moving under the immerse body of the ice barrier.

At three in the morning of the following

day, I was, awakened by a severe jolt. I sat up in bed and was immediately pitched into the middle of the room by another jolt. In alarm, I groped my way across the steeply tilted floor of the ship to the salon, where I found everything in complete disorder. Furniture and pictures were thrown about the room, although fortunately the instruments, securely fastened, were in place. The *Nautilus,* was listing heavily to the starboard bow.

I heard footsteps, and a confusion of voices, but Captain Nemo did not appear. Then Ned Land and Conseil entered the salon.

"Do you know what has happened?" I asked.

"We came to ask the master," replied Conseil.

"I know well enough!" exclaimed the Canadian. "The *Nautilus* has struck. And judging by the way she lies, I do not think she will get clear as she did that time in Torres Straits."

"That is hard to say until we have more facts," I said. "Let us see if at least she has come to the surface of the sea."

We went over to look at the manometer. It showed us to be at a depth of more than 180 fathoms! We had gone even deeper than before.

"Well, we must ask Captain Nemo," I said, trying to remain calm.

We looked in the library but he was not there. Then I thought that he must be in the pilot's cage. We would wait for him in the salon, to which we returned.

After twenty minutes Captain Nemo entered, but he seemed not to see us. His face, generally so impassive, showed signs of uneasiness. He looked at the compass silently, and then at the manometer. Going to the planisphere, he placed his finger in the region of the antarctic. I would not interrupt him, but some minutes later, when he turned toward me, I said, using one of his own expressions in the Torres Straits, "An incident, Captain?"

"No, sir; an accident this time. An enormous block of ice, a whole mountain, has turned over," he replied. "When some icebergs are undermined at their base by warmer water, by repeated collisions, their center of gravity changes, and the whole thing tilts over. This is what has happened tonight. In the process, a huge pinnacle of ice broke off and fell, striking the *Nautilus*, then gliding under its hull. It now holds the *Nautilus* in a tilted position."

"But can we not free the *Nautilus* by emptying its tanks so that it may right itself?"

"That, sir, is being done at this moment. You can hear the pump working. Look at the needle of the manometer — it shows that the *Nautilus* is rising. But the ice below is rising with it. Until the ice moves off, our position cannot be altered."

Indeed, the *Nautilus* still held the same position to the starboard bow. Doubtless it would right itself. But at this moment who knew if we might not be frightfully crushed between the ice below us and the iceberg above us?

Captain Nemo never took his eyes off the manometer. Since the ice had fallen, the *Nautilus* had risen about a 150 feet, but it still maintained the same perilous angle. Suddenly, there was a heavy sliding sound, and the *Nautilus* gradually shifted with a rolling motion. With relief, I noticed that the walls were nearly upright. With beating hearts we waited and felt the floor leveling itself under our feet.

"At last we have righted!" I exclaimed.

"Yes," said Captain Nemo, opening the panels of the salon.

We were floating free although still submersed in the water. The *Nautilus* was now imprisoned in a regular tunnel of ice about twenty yards wide, that must run through the iceberg itself! On either side of us towered dazzling walls of ice that glistened and sparkled like beds of emeralds, sapphires and diamonds.

It seemed that it would be easy now to move

forward through this ice tunnel and then dive deeper and make a free passage under the ice barrier.

It was then five in the morning, and at that moment a shock was felt at the bows of the *Nautilus*. I realized that its spur had struck. It must have been an error in maneuvering, I thought, for this underwater tunnel obstructed here and there by ice, was difficult to navigate. I expected Captain Nemo to free the spur and then continue forward. It did not seem possible that the tunnel could be entirely blocked. But, contrary to my expectations, the *Nautilus* took a decided retrograde motion.

"We are going backward," said Conseil.

"Yes," I replied. "Evidently this end of the tunnel has no outlet. We must go back again, and go out at the southern opening. That is all."

In speaking thus, I wished to appear more confident than I really was.

Many hours passed. How often I looked at the instruments hanging from the partition! The manometer showed that the *Nautilus* kept at a constant depth of more than 900 feet. The compass still pointed due south.

Then, at 8:25 A.M. there was a second collision. This time the stern had struck. I turned pale. My companions came closer and I took Conseil by the hand. Our looks betrayed our thoughts.

At this moment the captain entered the salon. I went to him quickly.

"Our course is barred southward?" I asked him.

"Yes, sir. The ice has shifted, and closed every outlet."

"We are blocked up, then?"

"Yes, sir, we are."

WANT OF AIR

THUS, around the *Nautilus*, above and below, was an impenetrable wall of ice that could hold us prisoners forever! I gazed steadily at the captain.

"Gentlemen," he said calmly, "there are two ways of dying, in the circumstances in which we are placed. The first is to be crushed; the second, to die of suffocation. Let us, then, calculate our chances."

"As to suffocation, Captain," I replied, "that is not to be feared, because our tanks of air are full."

"Just so. But they will only yield two days' supply of air. Now, for thirty-six hours we have been under water. Already the heavy atmosphere of the *Nautilus* requires renewal. In forty-eight hours our reserve will be exhausted."

"Well, Captain, can we be delivered before forty-eight hours?"

"We will attempt it, at least," he said. "I am going to sink the *Nautilus* to the ice below us, and my men will attempt to break through the ice floor to open sea."

Captain Nemo went out. Soon I discovered by a hissing noise that water was entering the tanks. The *Nautilus* sank slowly, and rested on the lower ice. We were now at a depth of 350 yards under water.

"My friends," I said to my companions, "our situation is grave, but I rely on your courage and energy."

"Sir," replied the Canadian, "I am ready to do anything for the general safety."

"Good!" and I held out my hand to the Canadian.

"I will add," he continued, "that I am as handy with the pickaxe as with the harpoon; if I can be useful to the captain, he can command my services."

"He will not refuse your help. Come, Ned!"

I led him to the room where the crew of the *Nautilus* were putting on their gear. I told the captain of Ned's proposal, which he accepted.

I left them and re-entered the salon, where the panels were open. Some moments later, Conseil and I saw Captain Nemo and a dozen of the crew with Ned Land set foot on the ice outside. They were armed with pickaxes and other ice-cutting equipment.

Before proceeding, Captain Nemo made soundings of the lower surface. As he told me later, a 30-foot plate of solid ice separated us from the open water beneath. It would be necessary to cut out a piece equal in size to the waterline of the *Nautilus*. Digging around the *Nautilus* would have involved considerable difficulty. So Captain Nemo planned to dig a trench in the ice off the port bow.

We must start work immediately if we were to reach free water in time to save ourselves.

After several hours' hard work, Ned Land came in exhausted. He and his comrades were replaced by new workers, whom Conseil and I joined.

When I re-entered, after working my shift, to take some food and rest, I noticed the difference between the pure air supplied by the air tank, and the atmosphere of the *Nautilus*. The air had not been renewed now for forty-eight hours.

After twelve hours' work we had removed a layer of ice only one yard thick, or a total of about 650 cubic yards! Reckoning that it took twelve hours to accomplish this much, it would take at least five nights and four days to bring this enterprise to a satisfactory conclusion. Five nights and four days — and only enough air in the tanks for two days! The situation was terrible. But everyone had faced the danger squarely, and each was determined to do his duty to the end.

On the morning of March 26th, when I joined the work crew, I noticed that the side walls had thickened visibly and were gradually closing in. If this continued we would all be crushed, even inside the *Nautilus*. Could anything be done to stop the closing walls of ice? I did not think so.

There seemed no point in telling my companions of this new danger. What was the good of weakening their efforts and the determination they displayed in their painful work of escape? But when I went on board again, I told Captain Nemo of this grave complication.

"I know it," he said, in that calm tone which

could counteract the most terrible fears. "It is one danger more."

"How long will the air in the reservoirs last for us to breathe on board?" I asked.

The captain looked in my face. "After tomorrow they will be empty!"

A cold sweat came over me. Even now, as I write, my recollection is still so vivid, that an involuntary terror seizes me, and my lungs seem to be without air.

Meanwhile Captain Nemo reflected silently, and evidently an idea had struck him.

"Boiling water!" he muttered.

"Boiling water?" I cried.

"Yes, sir. We are enclosed in a space that is relatively confined. Would not jets of boiling water, constantly injected by the pumps, raise the temperature in this part, and stay the freezing process? Let us try, Professor."

The thermometer then stood at eighteen degrees outside. Captain Nemo took me to the galleys, where the machines stood that furnished the drinkable water by evaporation. They filled these with water. And in a few minutes the heating coils brought this water to 212°F. It was directed toward the pumps, and cold water, drawn from the sea, replaced the water which came boiling from the coils into the body of the pump. The injection was begun, and three hours later the outside thermometer registered twenty degrees above zero. In two hours, it was twenty-four degrees.

"We shall succeed," I said to the captain.

"I think," he answered, "that we shall not be crushed. Now we have only suffocation to fear."

During the night the temperature of the water rose to thirty degrees. Since sea water only freezes at 28.4°F. there might now even be some melting action to help us in our work.

By the next day, March 27th, so much ice had been removed that four yards only remained to be cleared away. But that was forty-eight hours' work, and air could not be renewed in the interior of the *Nautilus*.

This day the atmosphere became much worse. An intolerable weight oppressed me. Toward three o'clock in the afternoon, this feeling rose to a violent degree. Yawns dislocated my jaws. I gasped and my throat burned as I inhaled the poisonous air.

Yet, all this time, no one prolonged his voluntary task to take advantage of the breathing apparatus we wore as we worked. Each man handed in turn to his panting companion the air tank that supplied him with life. Captain Nemo set the example, and submitted first to this severe discipline. When the time came, he gave up his apparatus to another, and returned on board, calm, unflinching, unmurmuring.

That day the ordinary work was accomplished with unusual vigor. Only two yards remained to be raised from the surface. Two yards only separated us from the open sea. But the reservoirs were nearly emptied of air. The little that remained had to be kept for the workers — not a particle for the *Nautilus*. When I went back on board, I was half suffocated.

This was the sixth day of our imprisonment, and was to be our last. For Captain Nemo, realizing that the pickaxes and other small equipment worked too slowly, resolved to crush the icebed that still separated us from the open water. I marveled that this man's coolness and energy never forsook him. He could subdue his physical pains by the force of his morale.

By his orders the *Nautilus* was lightened, that is to say, raised from the icebed by a change of specific gravity until it floated right over the immense trench we had dug for its escape. Then the captain ordered the tanks to be filled with sufficient water to lower the *Nautilus* into the trench.

All the crew came on board, and the double

door of communication was shut. The *Nautilus* now rested on the ice which was not one yard thick, and which the sounding leads had perforated in a thousand places. The taps of the water tanks were then opened, and a hundred cubic yards of water were sucked in to increase the weight of the *Nautilus* to the needed tonnage. We waited, we listened, forgetting our sufferings in hope. Our safety depended on this last chance. I heard the humming sound under the hull. The ice cracked with a noise like tearing paper magnified many times, and the *Nautilus* sank.

"We are off!" murmured Conseil in my ear.

I could not answer him. I seized his hand and pressed it hard. All at once, carried away by its frightful overcharge, the *Nautilus* sank like a bullet under the waters. Then all the electric force was put on the pumps, that soon began to push the water out of the tanks.

After some minutes, we stopped our descent, and the manometer indicated a rising movement. The screw, going at full speed, made the iron hull tremble to its very bolts, and drew us toward the north. But if this floating under the iceberg lasted another day, I would be dead before we reached the open sea.

Half stretched upon a divan in the library, I

was suffocating. My face was purple, my lips blue. I neither saw nor heard. All notion of time had gone from my mind. My muscles could not contract. I do not know how many hours passed, but I felt as if I was going to die. Suddenly I came to. Some breaths of air penetrated my lungs. Had we risen to the surface of the waves? Were we free of the iceberg? No. Ned and Conseil, my two brave friends, were sacrificing themselves to save me. Some air still remained at the bottom of one apparatus. Instead of using it, they had kept it for me, and while they were being suffocated, they gave me life, drop by drop. I wanted to push back the thing. They held my hands, and for some moments I breathed freely.

I looked at the clock. It was eleven in the morning. It ought to be the 28th of March. The *Nautilus* streaked along at forty knots. It literally tore through the water. Where was Captain Nemo? Had he succumbed? Were his companions dead with him?

The manometer indicated that we were not more than three feet from the surface! A mere plate of ice separated us from the atmosphere; could we not break it? Perhaps. In any case the *Nautilus* was going to attempt it. I felt that it was slanting upward. Then, impelled by its powerful screw, it attacked the ice-field from beneath like a formidable battering-ram. It broke it by backing and then rushing forward against the field, which gradually gave way. At last, dashing suddenly against it, the *Nautilus* shot forward, crushing the icy field as it went. The hatch was opened — one might say torn off — and the pure air came in in abundance to all parts of the *Nautilus*.

FROM CAPE HORN TO THE AMAZON

How I GOT onto the platform, I have no idea. Perhaps the Canadian had carried me there. But I breathed, I inhaled sea air. We could draw this air freely into our lungs, and it was the breeze, the breeze alone, that filled us with this keen enjoyment.

The first words I spoke were words of gratitude and thankfulness to my two companions. Ned and Conseil had prolonged my life during the last hours of this long agony. All my gratitude could not repay such devotion.

"My friends," said I, "we are bound one to

the other forever, and I am under infinite obligations to you."

"Which I shall take advantage of!" exclaimed the Canadian.

"What do you mean?" said Conseil.

"I mean that I shall take you with me when I leave this infernal *Nautilus*."

"Well," said Conseil, "after all this, are we going right?"

"Yes," I replied, "for we are going the way of the sun, and now the sun is in the north."

"No doubt," said Ned Land; "but it remains to be seen whether the captain will bring the ship into the Pacific or the Atlantic Ocean — that is, into frequented or deserted seas."

I could not answer that, but I feared that Captain Nemo would rather take us to the vast ocean that touches the coasts of Asia and America at the same time. He would thus complete the tour round the submarine world, and return to those waters in which the *Nautilus* could sail freely.

The *Nautilus* went at a rapid pace. The polar circle was soon passed, and the course was set for Cape Horn. We were off that point of South America on March 31st, at seven o'clock in the evening. All our past sufferings were forgotten. The remembrance of that imprisonment in the ice was erased from our minds. We only thought of the future.

Captain Nemo did not appear again either in the salon or on the platform. The point shown each day on the planisphere, and marked by the lieutenant, showed me the exact direction of the *Nautilus*. To my great satisfaction, we were going back to the north by way of the Atlantic. The next day, April 1st, when the *Nautilus* rose to the surface some minutes before noon, we sighted land to the west. It was Terra del Fuego, which the first navigators named thus from seeing the quantity of smoke that rose from the natives' huts.

We had now covered 16,000 miles since our embarkation in the Seas of Japan!

About eleven o'clock in the morning the Tropic of Capricorn was crossed on the thirty-seventh meridian. We went at a giddy speed, and the natural curiosities of these seas passed too rapidly for observation.

But, on the 11th of April the *Nautilus* rose suddenly. The land which appeared was at the mouth of the Amazon River. We had crossed the equator. Twenty miles to the west were the Guianas, a French territory, on which we could have found an easy refuge. But a stiff breeze was blowing, and the furious waves would now have engulfed a small boat. Ned Land understood that, no doubt, for he spoke not a word about it. For my part, I did not mention his schemes of flight, for I would not urge him to make an attempt that must inevitably fail. I made the time pass pleasantly in interesting studies. During the days of April 11th and 12th, the *Nautilus* did not leave the surface of the sea, and the net brought in a marvelous haul of zoophytes, fish and reptiles.

The next day, April 12th, the *Nautilus* approached the Dutch coast, near the mouth of the Maroni. There several groups of sea cows herded together. They were manatees, peaceable and inoffensive sea animals, from eighteen to twenty-one feet in length. I told Ned Land and Conseil that provident Nature had assigned an important *role* to these mammals. Indeed, they, like the seals, are designed to graze on the submarine prairies, and thus destroy the accumulation of weed that obstructs the tropical rivers.

This day's fishing brought to a close our stay on the shores of the Amazon, and by nightfall the *Nautilus* had regained the high seas.

THE GIANT SQUID

On April 16th, we sighted Martinique and Guadaloupe, from a distance of about thirty miles out to sea. I glimpsed their tall peaks for but an instant. The Canadian, who was counting on landing at those French islands, or hailing one of the numerous inter-island boats, was quite disheartened. But so far from land, escape could not be thought of.

The Canadian, Conseil, and I had a long conversation on this subject. For six months we had been prisoners on board the *Nautilus*. We had now traveled 17,000 leagues; and, as Ned Land said, there was no reason why it should not come to an end. We could hope for no help from the captain of the *Nautilus*, only from ourselves.

Besides, for some time past Captain Nemo had become graver, more retired, less sociable. He seemed to shun me. I met him rarely. Formerly, he was pleased to explain the submarine marvels to me. Now he left me to my studies, and came no more to the salon. What change had come over him? For what cause?

But aside from that, I did not wish to bury with me my curious and novel studies. I had now the knowledge to write the true book of the sea. And this book, sooner or later, I wished to publish.

It was about eleven o'clock in the morning when Ned Land drew my attention to a large mass of seaweeds floating outside the panels.

"Well," I said, "these are proper hiding places for giant squid, and I should not be astonished to see some of these monsters."

"I will never believe that such animals exist," said Ned.

"When it is a question of monsters, the imagination is apt to run wild," I said.

"It is supposed that these squid can draw down vessels. The ancient naturalists speak of monsters whose mouths were like gulfs, and which were too large to pass through the Straits of Gibraltar."

"But how much is true of these stories?" asked Conseil.

"Nothing, my friends; at least of that which passes the limit of truth to get to fable or legend. But one cannot deny that squid of a large species exist. According to the calculations of some naturalists, one of these animals, only six feet long, would have tentacles twenty-seven feet long. That would suffice to make a formidable monster."

"Tell me, master, its head," asked Conseil, "is it not crowned with eight tentacles, that beat the water like a nest of serpents?"

"Precisely."

"Have not its eyes, placed at the back of its head, considerable development?"

"Yes, Conseil."

"And is not its mouth like a parrot's beak?"

"Exactly, Conseil."

"Very well! no offense to master," he replied, quietly; "if this is not a squid, then it is, at least, one of its brothers."

I looked at Conseil. Ned hurried to the window.

"What a horrible beast!" he cried.

I looked in my turn, and could not repress a

gesture of disgust. Before my eyes was a horrible monster, worthy of the ancient legends. It was eight yards long. It swam crossways in the direction of the *Nautilus* with great speed, watching us with its enormous staring green eyes. Its arms, or rather feet, fixed to its head, were twice as long as its body, and were twisted like the Furies' hair. One could see the air-holes on the inner side of the tentacles. The monster's mouth, a horned beak like a parrot's, opened and shut vertically. Its tongue, a horned substance, furnished with several rows of pointed teeth, came out quivering from this veritable pair of shears. Its body formed a fleshy mass that might weigh 4000 to 5000 pounds. The varying color changed with great rapidity, and passed successively from livid gray to reddish brown. What irritated this monster? No doubt the presence of the *Nautilus,* more formidable than itself, and on which its suckers or its jaws had no hold. Yet, what monsters these giant squid are! What vigor there is in their movements! Chance had brought us in its presence and I did not wish to lose the opportunity of carefully studying this specimen. I overcame the horror that inspired me; and, taking a pencil, began to draw it.

By this time other squid appeared at the port

light. I counted seven. They formed a procession after the *Nautilus*, and I heard them against the iron hull. I continued my work. These monsters kept pace with us in the water with such precision, they seemed immovable. Suddenly the *Nautilus* stopped. A shock made it tremble in every plate.

"Have we struck anything?" I asked.

"In any case," replied the Canadian, "we shall be free, for we are floating."

The *Nautilus* was floating, no doubt, but it did not move. A minute passed. Captain Nemo, followed by his lieutenant, entered the drawing room. I had not seen him for some time. He seemed dull. Without noticing or speaking to us, he went to the panel, looked at the squid, and said something to his lieutenant. The latter went out. Soon the panels were shut. The ceiling was lighted. I went toward the captain.

"A curious collection of squid?" I said.

"Yes, indeed, Mr. Naturalist," he replied, "and we are going to fight them, man to beast."

I looked at him. I thought I had not heard aright.

"Man to beast?" I repeated.

"Yes, sir. The screw is stopped. I think that

276

a squid is entangled in the blades. That is what prevents our moving."

"What are you going to do?"

"Rise to the surface, and slaughter this vermin."

"A difficult enterprise."

"Yes, indeed. The electric bullets are powerless against the soft flesh, where they do not find resistance enough to go off. But we shall attack them with the hatchet."

"And the harpoon, sir," said the Canadian, "if you do not refuse my help."

"I will accept it, Master Land."

"We will follow you," I said, and together we went toward the central staircase.

There, about ten men with boarding hatchets were ready for the attack. Conseil and I took two hatchets. Ned Land seized a harpoon. The *Nautilus* had then risen to the surface. One of the sailors, posted on the top ladder step, unscrewed the bolts of the panels. But hardly were the screws loosed, when the panel rose with great violence, evidently drawn by the suckers of a squid's arm. Immediately one of these arms slid like a serpent down the opening, and twenty others were above. With one blow of the axe, Captain Nemo cut this formidable tentacle; it slid wriggling down the ladder. Just as we were pressing one on the other to reach the platform, two other arms, lashing the air, came down on the seaman placed before Captain Nemo, and lifted him up with irresistible power. Captain Nemo uttered a cry, and rushed out. We hurried after him.

What a scene! The unhappy man, seized by the tentacle and fixed to the suckers, was balanced in the air at the caprice of this enormous monster. He rattled in his throat, attempting to cry, "Help! help!" Those words, *spoken in French*, startled me! I had a fellow countryman on board, perhaps several! That heartrending cry! I shall hear it all my life.

The unfortunate man was lost. Who could rescue him from that powerful grasp? However, Captain Nemo had rushed to the squid, and with one blow of the axe had cut through one arm. His lieutenant struggled furiously against other monsters that crept on the flanks of the *Nautilus*. The crew fought with their axes. The Canadian, Conseil, and I, buried our weapons in the fleshy masses. A strong smell penetrated the atmosphere. It was horrible!

For one instant, I thought the unhappy man, entangled with the squid, would be torn from its powerful suction. Seven of the eight arms had been cut off. One only wriggled in the air, brandishing the victim like a feather. But just as Captain Nemo and his lieutenant threw themselves on it, the animal ejected a stream of black liquid. We were blinded with it. When the cloud dispersed, the squid had disappeared, and my unfortunate countryman with it. Ten or twelve squid now invaded the platform and sides of the *Nautilus*. We rolled pell-mell into the midst of this nest of serpents, that wriggled on the platform in the waves of blood and ink. It seemed as though these slimy tentacles sprang up like hydra heads. Ned Land's harpoon, at each stroke, plunged into the staring eyes of the squid. But my bold companion was suddenly overturned by the tentacles of a monster he had not been able to strike.

Ah! how my heart beat with emotion and horror! The formidable mouth of a squid was open over Ned Land. The unhappy man would be cut in two. I rushed to his aid. But Captain Nemo was before me. His axe disappeared between the two enormous jaws, and, miraculously saved, the Canadian, rising, plunged his harpoon deep into its heart.

"I owed myself this revenge!" said the captain to the Canadian.

Ned bowed without replying. The combat had lasted a quarter of an hour. The monsters, vanquished and mutilated, left us at last, and disappeared under the waves. Captain Nemo, covered with blood, nearly exhausted, gazed upon the sea that had swallowed up one of his companions, and great tears gathered in his eyes.

THE GULF STREAM — NO ESCAPE

THE TERRIBLE SCENE of April 20th, none of us can ever forget. I have written it under the influence of violent emotion. I have read it to Conseil and to the Canadian. They found it exact as to facts, but insufficient as to effect.

I have said that Captain Nemo wept while watching the waves. His grief was great. It was the second companion he had lost since our arrival on board, and what a death! That friend, crushed, stifled, bruised by the dreadful arms of a giant squid, pounded by his iron jaws, would not rest with his comrades in the peaceful coral cemetery! In the midst of the struggle, it was the despairing cry uttered by the unfortunate man that had torn my heart. The poor Frenchman, forgetting his conventional language, had taken to his own mother tongue to utter a last appeal! Among the crew of the *Nautilus,* associated with the body and soul of the captain, recoiling like him from all contact with men, I had a fellow countryman. Did he alone represent France in this mysterious association, evidently composed of individuals of many nationalities?

It was one of those problems that rose up unceasingly before my mind!

Captain Nemo entered his room, and I saw him no more for some time. But that he was sad and unsettled I could see by the vessel, of which he was the soul, and which received all his impressions. The *Nautilus* did not keep on in its settled course. It floated about like a corpse at the will of the waves. It moved at random. Evidently the captain could not tear himself away from the scene of the last struggle, from this sea that had devoured one of his men. Ten days passed thus.

It was not till the 1st of May that the *Nautilus* resumed its northerly course, after having sighted the Bahamas. We were then following the current of the largest river in the sea — it has its own banks, fish, and its own warm temperatures. I mean the Gulf Stream. It really is a river — a salt river, even saltier than the surrounding Atlantic. Its average breadth is ten miles. In certain places the current flows with the speed of two and a half miles an hour.

It was on this ocean river that the *Nautilus* now sailed. And this current carried with it all kinds of living things. During the night, the phosphorescent waters of the Gulf Stream rivaled the electric power of our watchlight.

May 8th, we were passing Cape Hatteras, on the North Carolina coast. The *Nautilus* was still moving at random; all supervision seemed abandoned. I thought that, under these circumstances, escape would be possible. Indeed, the American shores offered an easy refuge anywhere.

Besides, the sea was a crossroads for steamers that ply between New York or Boston and the Gulf of Mexico; and day and night little schooners passed above us. We could hope to be picked up when we surfaced. It was a favorable opportunity.

One unfortunate circumstance thwarted the Canadian's plans. The weather was very bad. Tempests were frequent, and so were hurricanes. To attempt the rough sea in a frail boat was certain destruction. Ned Land admitted this, but he fretted, seized with an unhappiness that only flight could cure.

"Professor," he said to me, "this must come to an end. This Nemo is leaving land and heading north. But I declare to you, I have had enough of polar ice at the South Pole, and I will not follow him to the north."

"What is to be done, Ned, since flight is not practicable just now?"

"We must speak to the captain," he said. "You said nothing when we were in your native seas. I will speak, now we are in mine. When I think that before long the *Nautilus* will be near the St. Lawrence River — my river — near Quebec, my native town! Well, it makes me furious. Sir, I would rather throw myself into the sea! I will not stay here! I am stifled!"

The Canadian was evidently losing all patience. His vigorous nature could not stand this prolonged imprisonment. His face had altered. He had become more surly.

I knew what he must suffer. Nearly seven months had passed without our having had any news from land. And Captain Nemo's isolation, his altered spirits, especially since the fight with the squid, his silence, all made me view things in a different light.

"Well, sir?" said Ned, seeing I did not reply.

"Well, Ned! do you wish me to ask Captain Nemo his intentions concerning us?"

"Yes, sir."

"Although he has already made them known?"

"Yes; I wish it settled finally. Speak for me, in my name only, if you like."

"But I so seldom meet him. He avoids me."

"That is all the more reason for you to go to see him."

I resolved I would do so, and immediately went to his door and knocked. No answer. I knocked again, then turned the handle and went in. The captain was there, bent over his worktable; he had not heard me. Determined not to go without having spoken, I approached him. He raised his head quickly, frowned and said roughly, "You here! What do you want?"

"To speak to you, Captain."

"But I am busy, sir. I am working. I leave you at liberty to shut yourself up. Cannot I be allowed the same?"

This reception was not encouraging, but I was determined. "Sir," I said, coldly, "I have to speak to you on a matter that admits of no delay."

"What is that, sir?" he replied, ironically.

"Have you discovered something that has escaped me, or has the sea delivered up any new secrets?"

Before I could reply, he showed me an open manuscript on his table and said in a more civil tone, "Here, Professor, is a manuscript written in several languages. It contains the sum of my studies of the sea — and if it please God, it shall not perish with me. This manuscript, signed with my name, complete with the history of my life, will be shut up in a little unsinkable case. The last survivor of all of us on board the *Nautilus* will throw this case into the sea, and it will go whither it is borne by the waves."

The man's real name! His history, the story of his life! Then his mystery *would* be revealed some day. Would I be there to read it, I wondered.

"Captain," I said, "I can but approve of your intent. The result of your studies must *not* be lost. But the means you employ seems to me to be primitive. Who knows where the winds will carry this case, and into whose hands it will fall? Could you not use some other means? Could not you, or one of your . . ."

"Never, sir!" he said, interrupting me.

"But I and my companions are ready to keep

this manuscript in store. And, if you will put us at liberty . . ."

"At liberty?" said the captain, rising.

"Yes, sir. That is the subject on which I wish to question you. For seven months we have been here on board, and I ask you today, in the name of my companions and me, if your intention is to keep us here always?"

"Professor, I will answer you today as I did seven months ago: whoever enters the *Nautilus* must never quit it."

"You impose actual slavery on us!"

"Give it what name you please."

"But everywhere the slave has the right to regain his liberty."

"Who denies you this right? Have I ever tried to chain you with an oath?"

He looked at me with his arms crossed.

"Sir," I said, "to return a second time to this subject will be neither to your taste nor mine. But as we have entered upon it, let us follow through. I repeat, it is not only myself whom it concerns. Study is to me a relief, a diversion, a passion that could make me forget everything. Like you, I am willing to live in obscurity in the frail hope of bequeathing one day, to future time, the result of my labors. But it is otherwise with Ned Land. Every man worthy of the name deserves some consideration. Have you thought that love of liberty, hatred of slavery, can give rise to schemes of revenge in a nature like the Canadian's?"

Captain Nemo rose. "What Ned Land thinks of, attempts or tries — what does it matter to me? I did not seek him! It is not for *my* pleasure that I keep him on board! As for you, Professor, you are one of those who can understand everything, even silence. I have nothing more to say to you. Let this first time you have come to treat of this subject be the last, for a second time I will not listen to you."

I retired. Our situation was critical. I related my conversation to my two companions.

"We know for sure now," said Ned, "that we can expect nothing from this man. The *Nautilus* is nearing Long Island. We will escape, whatever the weather may be."

But the sky became more and more threatening. Symptoms of a hurricane became manifest! Low clouds scudded overhead. The swollen sea rose in huge billows. The birds disappeared, with the exception of the petrels, those friends of the storm.

The tempest burst on the 18th of May, just as the *Nautilus* was floating off Long Island. Instead of fleeing to the ocean depths, Captain

Nemo, by an unaccountable whim, braved it at the surface, and having made himself fast, kept his place on the platform throughout the storm.

So again Ned Land was frustrated in his plans for escape.

Because of the storm, we had moved eastward once more. All hope of escape on the shores of New York or the St. Lawrence had faded away. And poor Ned, in despair, had isolated himself like Captain Nemo.

For some days, the *Nautilus* wandered first on the surface, amid fogs, and then beneath.

On the 28th of May, the *Nautilus* was not more than 120 miles from Ireland. Was Captain Nemo going to land on the British Isles? No. To my great surprise he headed past the English Channel toward Brest, on the coast of central France.

During the whole of the 31st of May, the *Nautilus* made a series of circles in the off shore waters, which greatly interested me. It seemed to be seeking a spot it had some trouble in finding. At noon, Captain Nemo himself came to work the ship's log. He spoke no word to me, but seemed gloomier than ever.

The next day, the 1st of June, the *Nautilus* continued the same process. It was evidently seeking some particular spot in the ocean. Captain Nemo took the sun's altitude as he had done the day before. The sea was beautiful, the sky clear. About eight miles to the east, a large vessel could be discerned on the horizon. No flag fluttered from its mast, and I could not discover its nationality. Some minutes before the sun passed the meridian, Captain Nemo took his sextant, and watched with great attention. The perfect calm of the water greatly helped the operation. The *Nautilus* was motionless; it neither rolled nor pitched.

I was on the platform when the altitude was taken, and the captain pronounced these words: "It is here."

He turned and went below. Had he seen the vessel which was changing its course and seemed to be nearing us? I could not tell. I returned to the salon. The panels closed, I heard the hissing of the water in the reservoirs. The *Nautilus* began to sink, following a vertical line, for its screw communicated no motion to it. Some minutes later it stopped at a depth of more than 420 fathoms, resting on the ground. The luminous ceiling was darkened, then the panels were opened, and through the glass I saw the sea brilliantly illuminated by the rays of our lantern for at least half a mile round us.

I looked to the port side, and saw nothing but an immensity of quiet waters. But to starboard, on the bottom appeared something which at once attracted my attention. One would have thought it a ruin buried under a coating of white shells, much resembling a covering of snow. Upon examining the mass attentively, I could recognize the ever thickening form of a vessel bare of its masts, which must have sunk. It certainly belonged to past times. This wreck, to be thus encrusted with the lime of the water, must already be able to count many years passed at the bottom of the ocean.

What was this vessel? Why did the *Nautilus* visit its tomb? Could it have been aught but a shipwreck which had drawn it under the water? I knew not what to think, when near me in a slow voice I heard Captain Nemo say:

"Sir, seventy-four years ago, day for day on this very spot, this vessel, after fighting heroically, losing its three masts, with the water in its hold, and the third of its crew disabled, preferred sinking with its 356 sailors to surrendering. Its colors nailed to the poop, it disappeared under the waves to the cry of 'Long live the Republic!'"

"The French ship *Avenger*!" I exclaimed.

"Yes, sir the *Avenger*! A good name!" muttered Captain Nemo, crossing his arms.

A HECATOMB

THE WAY this strange man pronounced the last words — the *Avenger* — impressed itself deeply on my mind.

My eyes did not leave the captain, who, with his hand stretched out to sea, was watching with a glowing eye the glorious wreck. Perhaps I was never to know who he was, from whence he came, or where he was going. But I saw a man who had a hatred — either monstrous or sublime — which time could never weaken.

Did this hatred still seek for vengeance? The future would soon teach me that. But now the *Nautilus* was rising slowly to the surface again. Soon a slight rolling told me that we were on the sea. At that moment a dull boom was heard. I looked at the captain. He did not move.

"Captain?" said I.

He did not answer. I left him and mounted the platform. Conseil and the Canadian were already there.

"Where did that sound come from?" I asked.

"It was a gunshot," replied Ned Land.

I looked in the direction of the vessel I had already seen. It was nearing the *Nautilus*, and we could see that it was putting on steam. It was within six miles of us.

"What is that ship, Ned?"

"By its rigging, and the height of its lower masts," said the Canadian, "I bet she is a ship of war. May it reach us, and, if necessary, sink this cursed *Nautilus*."

"Friend Ned," replied Conseil, "what harm can it do to the *Nautilus*? Can it attack it beneath the waves? Can it cannonade us at the bottom of the sea?"

"Tell me, Ned," said I, "can you recognize what country she belongs to?"

The Canadian squinted his eyes for better focus, and for a few moments stared fixedly at the vessel.

"No, sir," he replied, "I cannot, for she shows no colors. But I can declare she is a man-of-war, for a long pennant flutters from her main mast."

For a quarter of an hour we watched the ship steaming toward us. I could not, however, believe that she could see the *Nautilus* from that distance. Soon the Canadian informed me that she was a large armored ram. Thick black smoke was pouring from her two funnels. She advanced rapidly. If Captain Nemo allowed her to come close, there was a chance of salvation for us.

"Sir," said Ned Land, "if that vessel passes within a mile of us I shall dive into the sea, and I should advise you to do the same."

I did not reply to the Canadian's suggestion, but continued watching the ship. Whether English, French, American, or Russian, she would be sure to take us in if we could only reach her. Presently a puff of white smoke burst from the fore part of the vessel. Something splashed near the stern of the *Nautilus*, and shortly afterward a loud explosion struck my ear.

"What! they are firing at us!" I exclaimed.

"Sir," said Ned, "they have recognized the unicorn."

"But," I exclaimed, "surely they can see that we are men!"

"It is, perhaps, because of that," replied Ned Land.

Ned was right. Of course! Thanks to our Pacific search, they knew now what to believe about the "monster." No doubt, on board the *Abraham Lincoln*, when the Canadian struck the *Nautilus* with the harpoon, Commander Farragut had recognized in the supposed narwhal a submarine vessel, more dangerous than any supernatural cetacean. Yes, it must have been so. And on every sea they were now seeking this engine of destruction.

Terrible indeed, if, as we supposed, Captain Nemo employed the *Nautilus* in works of vengeance. On the night when we were imprisoned in that cell, in the midst of the Indian Ocean, had he not attacked some vessel? The man buried in the coral cemetery, had he not been a victim to the shock caused by the *Nautilus*? Yes, I repeat it, it must be so. One part of the mysterious existence of Captain Nemo had been unveiled; and, if his identity had not been recognized, at least, the nations united against him were no longer hunting a mysterious creature, but a man who had vowed a deadly hatred against them.

All the past rose before me. Instead of

friends on board the approaching ship, we could only expect pitiless enemies. But the shot rattled above us. Some of them struck the sea and ricocheted harmlessly. None touched the *Nautilus*.

The attacking vessel was not more than three miles from us. In spite of the serious cannonade, Captain Nemo did not appear on the platform. Yet if one shot had struck the shell of the *Nautilus*, it would have been fatal.

The Canadian then said, "Sir, we must do all we can to get out of this dilemma. Let us signal them. They will then, perhaps, understand that we are honest folks."

Ned Land took his handkerchief to wave in the air. He had scarcely displayed it, when he was struck down by an iron hand, and fell in spite of his great strength, upon the deck.

"Fool!" exclaimed the captain, "do you wish to be pierced by the spur of the *Nautilus* before it is hurled at this vessel?"

Captain Nemo was terrible to hear; he was still more terrible to see. His face was deadly pale. His pupils were fearfully dilated. He did not speak, he *roared,* as, with his body thrown forward, he gripped the Canadian by the shoulders. Then leaving him and turning his attention to the ship of war, whose shot was still raining around us, he exclaimed in a powerful voice, "Ah, ship of an accursed nation, you know who I am! I do not need your colors to know you by! Look and I will show you mine!"

And on the fore part of the platform Captain Nemo unfurled a black flag, similar to the one he had placed at the South Pole. At that moment a shot struck the *Nautilus* but glanced off and was lost in the sea.

Captain Nemo shrugged his shoulders. Addressing me he said shortly, "Go down, you and your companions, go down!"

"Sir," I exclaimed, "are you going to attack this vessel?"

"Sir, I am going to sink it."

"You will not do that!"

"I shall do it," he replied, coldly. "And I advise you not to judge me, sir. Fate had shown you what you ought not have seen. The attack has begun. Go down."

"What is this vessel?"

"You do not know? Very well! So much the better! Its nationality to you, at least, will be a secret. Go down!"

We could but obey. About fifteen of the sailors surrounded the captain, looking with implacable hatred at the vessel nearing them. One could feel that the same desire of vengeance was in every soul. I went down at the moment another projectile struck the *Nautilus*, and I heard the captain exclaim:

"Strike, mad vessel! You will not escape the spur of the *Nautilus*. But it is not here that you shall perish! I would not have your ruins mingle with those of the *Avenger*!"

I reached my room. The captain and his second had remained on the platform. The screw was set in motion, and the *Nautilus*, moving with speed, was soon beyond the reach of the ship's guns. But the pursuit continued, and Captain Nemo contented himself with keeping his distance.

About four in the afternoon, being no longer able to contain my impatience, I went to the central staircase. The panel was open, and I ventured onto the platform. The captain was still walking up and down with an agitated step. He was looking at the ship, which was five or six miles to leeward.

He was going around it like a wild beast, drawing it eastward in pursuit. But he did not yet attack.

I wanted to plead with him just once, but no sooner had I spoken to Captain Nemo than he bade me be silent. "I am the law, and I am the judge! I am the oppressed, and there is the oppressor! Through him I have lost all that I loved, cherished, and venerated — country, wife, children, father, and mother. I saw all perish! All that I hate is there! Say no more!"

I cast a last look at the man-of-war, which was putting on steam, and rejoined Ned and Conseil.

"We will flee!" I exclaimed.

"Good!" said Ned. "What is this vessel?"

"I do not know. But whatever it is, it will be sunk before night. In any case, it is better to perish with it, than be made accomplices in a retaliation, the justice of which we cannot judge."

"That is my opinion too," said Ned Land, coolly. "Let us wait for night."

Night arrived. Deep silence reigned on board. The compass showed that the *Nautilus* had not altered its course. It was on the surface, rolling slightly. My companions and I resolved to escape when the vessel should be near enough either to hear us or to see us. Once on board the ship, if we could not prevent the blow which threatened it, we could, at least, do all that circumstances would allow. Several times I thought the *Nautilus* was preparing for attack, but Captain Nemo contented himself with allowing the ship to approach, and then fled once more before it.

Part of the night passed without any incident. We watched the opportunity for action. We spoke little. Ned Land would have dived into the sea, but I forced him to wait. According to my idea, the *Nautilus* would attack the ship at her waterline, and then it would not only be possible, but easy to fly.

At three in the morning, full of uneasiness, I mounted the platform. Captain Nemo had not left it. He was standing at the forepart near his flag, which a slight breeze displayed above his head. He did not take his eyes from the vessel. The intensity of his look seemed to attract, and fascinate, and draw it onward. Yet in the peaceful moonlight, sky and ocean rivaled each other in tranquillity. As I thought of the deep calm of these elements compared with all those passions brooding within the *Nautilus* I shuddered.

The vessel was now within two miles of us, lured by that strange light which the *Nautilus* showed at night. I could see the vessel's green and red lights, and its white lantern hanging from the fore mast. Sparks flew from the funnels, shining in the atmosphere like stars.

I remained thus until six in the morning,

without Captain Nemo noticing me. The ship stood off about a mile and a half from us, and with the first dawn of day the firing began afresh.

The moment could not be far off when my companions and myself should forever leave this man. I was preparing to go down to remind them, when the second officer mounted the platform, accompanied by several sailors. Some steps were taken which might be called the signal for action. They were very simple. The iron balustrade around the platform was lowered, and the lantern and pilot cages were pushed within the shell until they were flush with the deck, so that the cigar-shaped vessel was not ready for action. I returned to the salon.

The *Nautilus* still floated, rising and falling with the motion of the waves. The salon was brightened by the red streaks of the rising sun, and this dreadful day of the 2nd of June had dawned.

At five o'clock the speed of the *Nautilus* was slackening, and I knew that it was allowing them to draw nearer. Besides, the reports could be heard more distinctly.

"My friends," said I, "the moment has come.

One grasp of the hand, and may God protect us!"

Ned Land was resolute, Conseil calm, myself so nervous that I knew not how to contain myself. We all passed into the library. But the moment I pushed the door opening onto the central staircase, I heard the panel above close sharply. The Canadian rushed onto the stairs, but I stopped him. A well-known hissing noise told me that the water was running into the tanks, and in a few minutes the *Nautilus* was some yards beneath the surface of the waves. I understood the maneuver. It was too late to act. The *Nautilus* did not wish to strike at the impenetrable part of the warship, but below her waterline, where metal covering no longer protected the hull.

We were again imprisoned, unwilling witnesses of the dreadful drama that was preparing. We had scarcely time to think. Taking refuge in my room, we looked at each other without speaking. A deep stupor had taken hold of my mind. Thought seemed to stand still. I was in a painful state of dread.

I waited, I listened, every sense merged in that of hearing!

The speed of the *Nautilus* increased. It was preparing to rush. The whole ship trembled. Suddenly I screamed. I felt the shock. And I felt the penetrating power of the steel spur. I heard rattlings and scrapings. But the *Nautilus*, carried along by its propelling power, passed through the mass of the vessel, like a needle through sailcloth!

I could stand it no longer. Mad, out of my mind, I rushed from my room into the salon. Captain Nemo was there, mute, and grimfaced. He was looking through the port panel. A large mass cast a shadow on the water. And that it might lose nothing of her agony, the *Nautilus* was going down into the abyss with her. Ten yards from me I saw the gashed hull through which the water was rushing with the noise of thunder, then I saw the double line of guns. The bridge was covered with black agitated shadows.

The water was rising. The poor creatures were crowding the ratlines, clinging to the masts, struggling under the water. It was a human ant-heap overtaken by the sea. Paralyzed, stiffened with anguish, eyes staring, I panted. Breathless and voiceless, I too was watching! An irresistible attraction glued me to the glass!

Suddenly, there was an explosion. Her ammunition had caught fire and blown up her decks. Then the unfortunate vessel sunk more rapidly. Her top mast, laden with victims, now appeared. Then her spars, bending under the weight of men. And last of all, the top of her main mast. Then the dark mass disappeared, and, with it the dead crew, was sucked down.

I turned to Captain Nemo. That terrible avenger, a perfect archangel of hatred, was still watching. When all was over, he turned to his room, opened the door and entered. I followed him with my eyes. On the end wall I saw the portrait of a woman still young, and two little children. Captain Nemo looked at them for some moments, stretched his arms toward them, and kneeling down burst into deep sobs.

THE LAST WORDS OF CAPTAIN NEMO

THE PANELS had closed on this frightful vision, but light had not returned to the salon. All was silence and darkness within the *Nautilus*. At tremendous speed, a hundred feet beneath the water, it was leaving this desolate spot. Where was it going? To the north or south? Where was the man fleeing to, after such dreadful revenge?

I had returned to my room, where Ned and Conseil had remained silent enough. I felt an insurmountable horror toward Captain Nemo. Whatever he had suffered at the hands of these men, he had no right to punish them in such a terrible way. He had made me, if not an accomplice, at least a witness of his vengeance.

At eleven the electric light reappeared as I passed into the salon. It was deserted. I consulted the different instruments. The *Nautilus* was traveling northward at the rate of twenty-five knots. On taking the bearings by the chart, I saw that we were repassing the mouth of the English Channel and that our course was hurrying us toward the northern seas at a frightful speed.

That night we crossed two hundred leagues of the Atlantic. The sea was in darkness until the rising of the moon. I went back to my room, and fell asleep only to wake from dreadful nightmares of the horrible scene of destruction. From that day, who could tell into what part of the North Atlantic the *Nautilus* would take us? And I do not know how much longer it might have lasted, had it not been for the catastrophe which ended this voyage.

Of Captain Nemo I saw nothing whatever now, nor of his second officer. Not a man of the crew was visible for an instant. The *Nautilus* was now almost continually under water. When we came to the surface to renew the air, the panels opened and shut mechanically. There were no more marks on the planisphere. I knew not where we were. And the Canadian, too, his strength and patience at an end, kept to his cabin. Conseil could not draw a word from him; and fearing that in a fit of madness he might kill himself, watched him with constant devotion.

One morning — what date it was I could not say — I had fallen into a heavy sleep toward the early hours of the morning — a sleep both painful and unhealthy — when I suddenly awoke. Ned Land was leaning over me, saying in a low voice, "We are going to escape."

I sat up.

"When shall we go?" I asked.

"Tonight. All inspection on board the *Nautilus* seems to have ceased. All appear to be stupefied. You will be ready, sir?"

"Yes. Where are we?"

"In sight of land. I took the reckoning this morning in the fog — it's twenty miles to the east."

"What country is it?"

"I do not know — but whatever it is, we will take refuge there."

"Yes, Ned, yes. We will flee tonight, even if the sea should swallow us up."

"This sea is bad, the wind violent, but twenty miles in that small boat of the *Nautilus* does not frighten me. Unknown to the crew, I have been able to procure food and some bottles of water."

"I will follow you."

"But," continued the Canadian, "if I am surprised, I will defend myself. I will force them to kill me."

"We will die together, friend Ned."

I had made up my mind to all. The Canadian left me. I reached the platform, on which I could with difficulty support myself against the shock of the waves. The sky was threatening but we must escape. I returned to the salon, fearing and yet hoping to see Captain Nemo, wishing and yet not wishing to see him. What could I have said to him? Could I hide the horror with which he inspired me? No. It was better that I should not meet him face to face; better to forget him. And yet . . .

How long that day seemed, the last that I should pass in the *Nautilus*. I remained alone. Ned Land and Conseil avoided speaking, for fear of betraying themselves. At six I dined, but I was not hungry. I forced myself to eat in spite of my disgust, that I might not weaken myself. At half-past six Ned Land came to my room, saying, "We shall not see each other again before our departure. At ten the moon will not yet have risen. We will profit by the darkness. Come to the boat. Conseil and I will wait for you."

The Canadian went out without giving me time to answer. Wishing to check the course of the *Nautilus*, I went to the salon. We were running N.N.E. at frightful speed. I looked around at Captain Nemo's unrivaled collection of natural wonders, and at the art treasures in this museum — all destined to perish at the bottom of the sea along with him who had formed it. Then I returned to my room.

I dressed myself in strong sea clothing. I collected my notes, placing them carefully about me. My heart beat loudly. I could not check its pulsations. Certainly my trouble and agitation would have betrayed me to Captain Nemo's eyes. What was he doing at this moment? I listened at the door of his room. I heard steps. Captain Nemo was there. He had not gone to rest. At every moment I expected him to appear and ask me why I wished to leave. I was constantly on the alert. My imagination magnified everything. The impression became at last so sharp that I asked myself if it would not be better to go to the captain's room, and face him with our resolve.

It was the inspiration of a madman. Fortunately, I resisted the desire and stretched myself on my bed to quiet my agitation. My nerves became somewhat calmer, but in my excited brain I saw over again all my existence on board the *Nautilus;* every incident which had happened since my disappearance from the *Abraham Lincoln* — the submarine hunt, the savages of Papua, the coral cemetery, Atlantis, the imprisonment in the ice at the South Pole, the fight with the giant squid, and the horrible scene of the unknown vessel sunk with all her crew. All these events passed before my eyes like scenes in a drama. Then Captain Nemo seemed to grow enormously, and to assume superhuman proportions.

It was half-past nine. I held my head between my hands to keep it from bursting. I closed my eyes, I would not think any longer. There was another half hour to wait, another half hour of waking nightmare to be lived through.

At that moment I heard the distant strains of the organ, a sad harmony — the wail of a soul longing to break these earthly bonds. I listened with every sense, scarcely breathing, plunged, like Captain Nemo, in that musical ecstacy which was drawing his spirit to the end of life.

Then a sudden thought terrified me. Captain Nemo had left his room. He was in the salon, which I must cross. He might see me, perhaps speak to me. A gesture or a single word from him might weaken my resolve to escape.

But ten o'clock was about to strike. The moment had come for me to leave my room and join my companions.

I must not hesitate, even if Captain Nemo himself should rise before me. I opened my door carefully. As it turned on its hinges, it seemed to make a dreadful noise.

I crept down the dark stairs of the *Nautilus*, stopping at each step to listen. I reached the door of the salon and opened it slightly. The room was in darkness and the deep strains of the organ told me that Captain Nemo was there. He did not hear me. Even in full light I do not think he would have noticed me, so entirely was he absorbed in his music.

I stole along the carpet, avoiding the slightest sound which might betray my presence. I was at least five minutes reaching the opposite side.

As I opened the door into the library, a sigh from Captain Nemo nailed me to the spot. I could faintly see him in the light from the library. He came toward me silently with his arms crossed, and I heard him murmur these words — the last which ever struck my ear:

"Almighty God! Enough! Enough!"

Was it a confession of remorse which thus escaped from this man?

In desperation I rushed through the library, mounted the central staircase, and finally reached the boat. I crept through the opening, which had already admitted my two companions.

"Let us go! Let us go!" I exclaimed.

"At once!" replied the Canadian.

The hatch of the *Nautilus* was first closed, then fastened down by a wrench, which Ned Land had himself, and the same tool was used to open the outside hatch. The Canadian proceeded to loosen the bolts which held the small boat to the submarine.

Suddenly a noise within was heard. Voices were answering each other loudly. What was the matter? Had they discovered our flight? I felt Ned Land slipping a dagger into my hand.

"Yes," I murmured, "we know how to die!"

Then we made out one word that chilled us — one word, many times repeated. The dreadful word revealed the cause of the agitation spreading on board the *Nautilus*. It was not ourselves the crew were thinking of!

"The maelstrom! the maelstrom!" I exclaimed.

The maelstrom! Could a more terrifying word in a worse situation have sounded in our ears! We were in the dangerous waters off the coast of Norway, where the tidal currents between the Faroe and Loffoden islands rush together with irresistible violence, forming a whirlpool from which no vessel ever escapes. From every point of the horizon enormous waves were meeting, forming a gulf justly called the "Navel of the Ocean," whose power of attraction extends to a distance of twelve miles. Not only vessels, but whales and polar bears from the far north are sucked down.

It was there that the *Nautilus*, voluntarily or involuntarily, had been run by the captain. The submarine was already running in a spiral, the circumference of which was rapidly lessening. And our boat, which was still fastened to the *Nautilus*'s side, was being carried along at a dizzying speed. I felt that sick giddiness which arises from long continued whirling.

Our horror was at its height. We were paralyzed with fear, and covered with the cold sweat of terrible agony! What dreadful noise! Roaring flung back in echoes from mountains miles away! In these waters the strongest bodies are

313

broken on the sharp rocks of its yawning abyss!

Our boat rocked frightfully. The *Nautilus*, its iron plates cracking, sometimes seemed to stand upright, and we with it!

"We *must* hold on," said Ned. "We may still be saved if we can stay with the *Nautilus*."

He had scarcely spoken these words when we heard a crashing noise. The bolts gave way, and our boat, torn from its groove, was hurled like a stone from a sling into the midst of the whirlpool!

My head struck a piece of iron, and with the violent shock I lost all consciousness.

CONCLUSION

THUS ENDS THE VOYAGE under the seas. What passed during that night — how the boat escaped from the eddies of the maelstrom — how Ned Land, Conseil, and myself ever came out of that terrible gulf — I cannot tell.

But when I returned to consciousness, I was lying in a fisherman's hut on the Loffoden Isles. My two companions, safe and sound, were near me holding my hands. We embraced each other heartily.

At that moment we could not think of returning to France. The means of communication between the north of Norway and the south are rare. And I was therefore obliged to

315

wait for the steamboat running monthly from Cape North.

And among the worthy people who have so kindly received us, I revise my record of these adventures once more. Not a fact has been omitted, not a detail exaggerated. It is a faithful narrative of this incredible expedition in an element inaccessible to man, but to which Progress will one day open a road.

Shall I be believed? I do not know. And it matters little, after all. What I now affirm is that I have a right to speak of these seas under which, in less than ten months, I have crossed 20,000 leagues in that submarine tour of the world, which has revealed so many wonders.

But what has become of the *Nautilus*? Did it somehow escape from the maelstrom? Does Captain Nemo still live? And does he still follow under the ocean those frightful retaliations?

Will the waves one day give up his manuscript containing the history of his life? Shall I ever know his name?

I hope that his powerful vessel conquered the sea at its most terrible gulf, and that the *Nautilus* survived where so many other vessels have been lost! If it be so — if Captain Nemo still inhabits the ocean — may hatred be appeased in that savage heart! May the contemplation of so many wonders extinguish forever the spirit of vengeance! If his destiny be strange, it is also sublime. Have I not understood it myself? Have I not lived ten months of this unnatural life? And to the question asked by Ecclesiastes 3000 years ago, "That which is far off and exceeding deep, who can find it out?" At least two men can give an answer:

CAPTAIN NEMO AND MYSELF.

THE END